35p Elt OAKLANDS HOUSE

99

)00

WINDS OF DESTINY

WINDS OF DESTINY

Pat Dalton

Chivers Press · G.K. Hall & Co.
Bath, Avon, England · Thorndike, Maine USA

This Large Print edition is published by Chivers Press, England, and by
G.K. Hall & Co., USA.

Published in 1996 in the U.K. by arrangement with the author

Published in 1995 in the U.S. by arrangement with Diamond Literary
Agency, Inc.

U.K. Hardcover ISBN 0–7451–3149–2 (Chivers Large Print)
U.S. Softcover   ISBN 0–7838–1455–0 (Nightingale Collection
                                                        Edition)

The text of this Large Print edition is unabridged.
Other aspects of the book may vary from the original edition.

Set in 16 pt. New Times Roman.

Printed in Great Britain on acid-free paper.

British Library Cataloguing in Publication Data available

Library of Congress Cataloging-in-Publication Data

Card Number: 95–77933

*To my grandmother, Mae Frederick Bottemer,
who instilled in me a love of reading, and to
my mother, Elzena Bottemer Wasson, who
was out working to support me at the time...*

CHAPTER ONE

The wind was hostile, relentless.

It compelled the rain to lash at Caryn Tallis' rented Toyota as if it were nothing more than a cockleshell amid a raging ocean. The storm seemed an enemy, violent and dangerous, yet cloaked with invisibility by the inky night.

The Lonely Isle, the Forgotten Isle, Molokai had been called in centuries past. And it seemed no less lonely and forgotten tonight than two hundred years ago, still guarded by the wind.

But Caryn recognized loneliness as the legacy of her chosen career, even for a male, more so for a woman in a 'man's profession.' And she had earned the right of assignment to remote, unfamiliar places such as Molokai, smallest and least developed of Hawaii's five major islands.

Wearily, Caryn brushed a straying strand of tawny hair away from her cheek. Her medium-length tresses had dried from their earlier rain-saturated state in the three hours since she'd determinedly headed in this direction from the small airport near the main town of Kaunakakai.

Had less than twenty hours passed since she'd left the corporate headquarters in Minneapolis? It seemed more like twenty days.

The lengthy plane trip had been further prolonged when Los Angeles International Airport was fogged in for several hours, delaying her connection to Honolulu. Fortunately—or perhaps unfortunately, Caryn now realized—the airline had arranged a private charter to ferry Caryn on to Molokai that night since she'd missed the last scheduled commercial flight.

Caryn slowed the car to a crawl as she encountered yet another stream crossing the main highway. She had braved the previous torrents. But this one, wider than the living room of her apartment in Minneapolis, flowed close to the red marker, the depth indicated by a warning sign as perilous.

Her blue eyes, already veiled by fatigue, attempted unsuccessfully to plumb the true depth of the dark, coursing water, to estimate its proportion to the automobile which she was now asking to double as a boat.

The Toyota's headlights were mere pinpricks in an endless void. Caryn had no idea what fringed either side of the narrow road.

If she pulled over to sleep in the car for the balance of the night, she risked being in the path of a flash flood or a crashing palm tree brought down on her by this intense storm. The Toyota seemed frighteningly tiny and fragile.

If she attempted to cross, the stream might sweep her to—where? Presumably, the ocean

2

lurked on her right.

The same single-minded determination prevailing through her last few years triumphed again. Some might call it stubbornness or even foolhardiness, Caryn acknowledged. With a wry shrug of her shoulders Caryn eased the Toyota into the stream, breathing an audible sigh of relief when she emerged on the opposite side.

Continuing through the ebony night, she swerved for what seemed the thousandth time—too late to miss another of the potholes in the highway, but a lucky turn anyway. Otherwise she wouldn't have noticed the small, unillumined sign swinging frantically on its hinges.

Caryn backed up slightly and swiveled left. The Toyota's beams confirmed she'd seen correctly.

WindsEnd, the battered sign proclaimed.

A misnomer if ever there was one.

Buoyed by nearing her destination, Caryn tried to dispel her exhaustion and urged the car along. But twenty miles per hour was the maximum speed safe in these adverse conditions, with visibility on the unfamiliar terrain limited to a few feet.

As she rounded another curve, a tall silhouette detached from the rest of the blackness—right in her path!

Caryn jerked the steering wheel to the left as she ground down on the brakes. Water and mud spewed beneath the tires as the car skidded off the pavement. The lone figure was thoroughly drenched, but otherwise unharmed.

Caryn launched herself out of the car the very second it came to a halt. 'Are you all right?!' she shouted anxiously, addressing the shadow scarcely seen in the vague reddish glow of the taillights.

The words weren't completely out of her mouth before a deep voice rumbled, 'What the heck are you doing speeding along here in the middle of the night!'

'I was only going twenty miles an hour,' Caryn defended, although quivery herself at the near miss. 'What were you doing in the middle of the road anyway?!'

'In the middle of my own driveway, you mean! Can't you tourists at least stick to the highway!'

'Look, I'm sorry. I couldn't see a thing in this storm. I must have taken a wrong turn. Can you direct me to WindsEnd?'

'Practically run a man down, then politely ask for directions...'

The voice, as inhospitable as the weather, nonetheless possessed an intriguing timbre, Caryn now noticed.

'The main house is to your right, but this plantation is *not* a tourist attraction.'

'Thank you. I imagine that's where I'll find Vance Warner.' She retrieved her purse from the car.

'What do you want with him?'

'Business. Mine, not yours.' Caryn was too tired for a verbal battle.

'Are you another reporter?'

'No, are you? You're the one asking all the questions.' Caryn trudged and sloshed her way toward the squares of light.

She rang the door chimes several times before annoyedly banging the brass knocker in the shape of a pineapple. Finally, the massive door swung back—as if opened by spirits on the wind. No one was visible. Only a dim strip of illumination penetrated from some room near the rear of the house.

'Hello?' she ventured.

'What do you want here?' The rumbling voice was the same she'd heard outside, but its owner remained barricaded behind the heavy door.

'Same as I told you out there. To see Vance Warner,' Caryn said frostily, 'on business—his and mine.'

'I handle all Mr Warner's business.'

Caryn shrugged resignedly. 'Okay. I'm Caryn Tallis with Resorts Inc., here for the construction project.'

'Where's your husband? Waiting in the warm, dry car?' The rumble was decidedly unfriendly.

'No.' She wasn't going to elaborate to this flunky. 'Look, I told you I'm sorry I drenched you in the driveway. You can send any cleaning bills to me,' she offered crisply, though she knew no sane person would wear anything unwashable in that downpour. 'I've had a long trip, and I'd like to get some rest. According to the contract, WindsEnd is to provide a guest cottage for the construction superintendent, and meals at the main house since the nearest restaurant is a two-hour drive. Now can I see Mr Warner?'

'Mr Warner wants to be disturbed as little as possible by this project.'

He didn't mind his bank account being disturbed by a few million dollars recently, Caryn fumed to herself.

The man grumbled an offer. 'I'll show you to the cottage. I suppose you expect me to carry your luggage?'

'Certainly not.'

'Suit yourself.'

Caryn wished she could suit herself, or dress herself. But her luggage was following a different itinerary, courtesy of the airline, and had not arrived on Molokai with her. The airline had promised they'd try to find and deliver her suitcases the next day.

As the man stepped forward, Caryn noticed that he towered above her, a phenomenon infrequently encountered at her own five feet eight inches. He didn't bother with a raincoat, but grabbed a large flashlight from a shelf on the *lanai*. Wordlessly, he led and she followed,

6

glad a stone path connected the two buildings, although shallow layers of mud had washed over it in some places.

He opened the cottage door and switched on the light. She saw that no mud caked his jeans. So he must have changed while he kept her waiting at the door of the main house.

His wet, thin cotton shirt clung to sizable muscles in his arms and back. The image of a Greek frieze flitting through Caryn's mind was reinforced when he turned to face her and she was confronted by the appreciable expanse of his chest.

She must be very tired, she decided. After all, she was used to being around men. Lots of them. And most of them had bulging muscles to match this man's.

Why did there seem to be something about him...? He turned to leave, saying, 'Breakfast is at six-thirty.'

When he moved sideways past her through the door, their bodies almost touched. Caryn dismissed her brief quickening of breath as a symptom of fatigue.

She was boosted by the pleasant interior of the cottage. It was nicer than many types of housing she expected to occupy on future projects for Resorts Inc. around the world. Those might range from a cramped hotel room to a lizard-infested hut to a leaky tent.

The cottage's decor of lemon yellow and white enhanced an impression of spaciousness.

7

Along the left front of the long, rectangular room arched a handsome black lavastone fireplace, faced by two armchairs, a table, and a reading lamp. Against the right wall stood a desk. A king-sized bed sporting a bright yellow spread commanded the far left corner, while a built-in white dresser, drawers, shelves, and closet were on the far right.

A pale yellow swirled pattern of tile covered the floor. A carpet would be impractical with such muddy surroundings.

Caryn was about to confirm that the small door at the back led to the bathroom when she was startled.

'I guess I should set a fire for you since tonight's unusually chilly,' the man mumbled begrudgingly.

'Thank you,' she said simply, welcoming a truce.

While he loaded wood into the fireplace, Caryn couldn't help admiring the ripple of muscles in his arms, across his shoulders, along taut thighs as he hunkered down.

Suddenly, she found herself gazing into cloudy gray eyes, fringed by long sun-tipped lashes. His thick reddish brown hair was highlighted by the spreading fire.

'I suppose I'll have to wait up for your husband to arrive in another car. This time I'll stay inside where it's safe, though.' His grumble broke the spell.

Reversing her mellowing thoughts, she

retorted, 'I don't have a husband. *I'm* the construction superintendent for the resort project.'

Surprise conquered his features for mere seconds. 'I see,' he acknowledged.

Caryn found herself searching his sculpted features, his silver eyes, for a clue to his genuine reaction. But none surfaced.

He left with a perfunctory 'Good night.'

Caryn eyed the bed with interest, hoping to be fresh and energetic for the construction project tomorrow and all the tomorrows thereafter. She was eager to prove her management abilities on her first major assignment as a construction superintendent for Resorts Inc. The company planned, designed, financed, and acted as its own prime contractor for large hotel complexes throughout the world.

Resolutely, she exorcised her demons of anxiety about the resistance she expected to encounter from some of the male employees, many of whom already had been hired by the assistant superintendent, who had himself been selected by her boss, Jordan Nash, on his last trip to Molokai.

Caryn had traveled as usual with only a briefcase accompanying her in the cabin of the airplane. Thus she lacked such basics as soap and toothpaste.

But she was mildly revived by the spray of the shower along her body, a form which she'd

9

always regarded as 'big built' though others had tried to convince her she was nicely and solidly put together in a way more attractive than she realized.

Her thoughts briefly detoured to another body. One clad in a clinging wet shirt. But she determined to shrug him from her mind.

She hoped Vance Warner wasn't as uncongenial as his assistant.

CHAPTER TWO

The rain had relented by the next morning, but gray clouds loitered menacingly below the tops of the hills.

Surprised to awaken at 6 A.M., tired as she had been from the trip, Caryn remembered her biological clock didn't realize yet that it had been transported from Minneapolis where the time was 10 A.M.

She didn't waste a moment debating what to wear, having no choice but to slip on the same peach linen slacks and paler peach silk blouse worn on the plane yesterday.

As she followed the mud-strewn path to the front door of the main house at six-thirty, a petite Asian woman who'd apparently been waiting for her at the side intercepted her. 'You the resort lady?'

'Yes, hello, I'm Caryn Tallis,' she introduced

10

pleasantly.

'The kitchen entrance is back here.' The woman turned, expecting to be followed.

So she was to be relegated to the rear door and meals in the kitchen! Well, the sales contract didn't specify where and under what circumstances she would receive meals. Considering her reception thus far, she could only hope for something more than gruel.

Attempting to adopt a more positive attitude, Caryn reminded herself that conditions on future assignments could be worse. She might dine on freeze-dried toast in the New Guinea jungle someday.

She noted in the light of early morning that the huge house was built of mortared black lava rock interspersed with white frame. A bright white, covered *lanai* encircled the lower floor of the entire structure, providing the base for a second-story balcony on the south side facing the ocean.

A profusion of vivid flowers, shrubs, and trees glorified the grounds. To the east, a large, crescent-shaped swimming pool curved within a grove of trees.

The Asian woman motioned her to a place at a small table in the spacious and functional kitchen. Caryn estimated the woman's age in the mid-forties, though it was difficult to tell. She wore a simple cotton shift, and only a few strands of silver interrupted the coal black hair pulled into a tight bun. Fixed up a bit, she

11

could be quite attractive.

'I am Hira. I am in charge of the house. Every morning you will get the same breakfast as Mr Warner and me,' Hira explained as she placed a plate containing bacon, eggs, and papaya in front of Caryn.

'Thank you,' Caryn said, genuinely grateful not to be confronted by gruel.

'Water's hot in the teakettle on the stove. Instant coffee, instant tea, and sugar are on the table.'

A whiff of brewed coffee from the room beyond tantalized Caryn's nostrils, but she helped herself to the instant. Hira turned her back and busied herself at the far end of the kitchen, staunching any further conversation.

Hira, like Vance Warner, his hulky assistant, and the weather, definitely could be dubbed unfriendly. Uncertain what was expected of her, Caryn delivered her dishes to the sink before starting to leave.

'Wait,' Hira ordered.

Caryn supposed she was expected to wash her dishes, and perhaps clean the cinders from a hearth somewhere.

'Your lunch is in the bag by the door.' Hira returned to her work.

Caryn felt like an unwelcome child being packed off to school as she picked up the sandwich and banana allotted for her next meal.

Her mood improved considerably, despite

the gusting wind and threatening clouds, as she walked the resort site. Caryn knew her boss, Jordan Nash, and the others in the real estate syndicate had negotiated with Vance Warner almost two years before finally succeeding in acquiring a parcel of his beachfront property. But despite special difficulties building in this remote area, the long-term profit potential was excellent. Molokai's appeal to tourists was escalating—particularly for those veteran travelers who'd already visited the other islands.

The Resorts Inc. site had much individual appeal also, a sliver of land along golden sands, with the neighboring island of Maui normally visible across azure waters. Today, though, the ocean was irascible gray.

The red hue of the earth came as no surprise to Caryn since she'd reviewed the soil analysis, but was delightful to view in person. She mused that Scarlett O'Hara complete with Tara could be happily transplanted here. Pink puddles punctuated the expanses between palms and other foliage.

Ruffled hills rising in the center of the island appeared fluted by the thumbs of the Jolly Green Giant. Silver sage mottled the ruby earth.

'What do you think of it?' His voice erupted to her left.

Remembering this man's attitude the previous evening, Caryn, turning toward him,

13

replied simply but directly, 'Do you really care what I think of it?'

'Of course not.' The slight smile on his lips teased her. 'Just making conversation.'

His eyes reflect the gray of the omnipresent clouds, the sage, today's sea, Caryn thought as she looked at him. And his hair seems tinged by the red earth of Molokai. As if he'd sprung from the island itself.

Her next comment sounded more mockingly formal than she'd intended. 'Please convey my thanks to Mr Warner for my breakfast and lunch.'

'All part of the contract. I see now why Nash was concerned about his construction superintendent not being just one of the boys and putting together some sort of meals along with the rest of the employees even after the temporary quarters are set up for the project.'

'The decision who would be superintendent on this project hadn't been finalized at the time the contract was negotiated,' she explained patiently. 'It can be difficult for the workers always to have their supervisor around. When would they get a chance to complain about the boss?'

'Ah, the loneliness of command,' he commented and probed at the same time.

'I'm accustomed to being alone, but never lonely,' Caryn clarified honestly.

'I can understand that,' he murmured before depersonalizing the course of the conversation.

'How about a lesson in Hawaiian to help you bark orders properly? On the islands we have special directions—*makai* means "toward the sea," *mauka* means "away from the sea."' His muscular arms gestured appropriately.

'If you went too far *mauka*, you'd be going *makai*,' Caryn confirmed her understanding. 'Just in case the need ever arises,' she continued sweetly, 'how do you say, "Go jump in the sea"?'

'You set an example by doing it first yourself.'

As if to urge her toward that very action, a sudden gust of wind nearly lifted her off her feet.

'That's unusual,' he observed. 'The winds here usually blow *mauka*.' Then the silver eyes glided over her. 'Perhaps after you get your directions straight, Vance Warner will ask you to join him for dinner some night.'

She responded with the same half-kidding sarcasm, 'I hope the excitement won't prove fatal.'

'I've been told some women find him exciting.'

'I meant the excitement for him, not for me.' Her voice remained deceptively demure.

Her verbal sparring partner threw back his head and laughed, his deep, delightful tones seeming to echo through the hills. Caryn's own laughter joined his, relieved that this round had ended.

15

The rain chose that moment to begin again, sputtering a warning of the impending downpour.

'You'd best get back to your cozy cottage, Ms. Tallis. Want me to light your fire again?'

'I can handle it. I'll even chop the wood myself if necessary.' With a smile she set him straight as to her self-sufficiency. Caryn Tallis didn't need anybody, didn't want to need anybody. She jogged toward shelter, leaving him behind.

The deluge continued through the day, so she reviewed the plans and blueprints for the resort while seated in front of her fireplace. The temperature didn't necessitate a fire, but the constantly changing flickers were mentally comforting and pacifying.

Bob Saito, the architect from Honolulu, was to fly in for a final check tomorrow. Then they'd begin clearing the land, working around some of the palms which had been reprieved to serve as part of the landscaping for the new resort.

Calling the airline at four-thirty from the telephone in the main kitchen, she learned that her baggage was having a fine time someplace without her, still not located. The nearest drugstore was a two-hour drive.

She asked Hira, 'Could I borrow some soap and toothpaste, and maybe a toothbrush if you have an extra?'

The housekeeper appeared tempted to point

out that supplying personal items was not part of the contract. But she nodded, left the room, and returned a few minutes later with the requested essentials. She responded to Caryn's expression of thanks with 'Dinner's at seven-thirty.'

Caryn entered the kitchen again at the appointed hour, ravenously hungry since her stomach hadn't adjusted to the new time.

Hira looked at her askance. 'I think Mr Warner expected you to dress for dinner with him,' she commented, more in surprise than in rebuke.

'I am definitely not *un*dressed, Hira,' Caryn pointed out politely, wearing her same, one-and-only outfit—now mud-streaked on the lower legs as well as generally disheveled. She was astonished that the old codger deigned to bear her company at a meal, but admitted to some interest in meeting this haughty fossil. However, she refused to acknowledge her curiosity as to whether his robust assistant would dine with them.

Hira ushered her through a swinging door into an elegant dining room with rich cherry-wood paneling on the walls and a simply designed but handsome crystal chandelier. Caryn assumed the drapes drawn along the south wall concealed glass doors with a view of the ocean, but now only blackness waited outside.

She did feel dowdy in this setting, but

refused to dwell on that. Caryn noted with disappointment that only two places were set at the long table, though both were at the same end to facilitate conversation.

'Announcing his lordship of the manorship, Mr Vance Warner,' the familiar voice boomed.

Really, this was a bit much—the expression on Caryn's face mirrored her thoughts.

Then her nemesis swept into the room, rakishly pulled out one of the chairs, and sat down. His gray eyes challenged her teasingly, 'You going to eat standing up?'

'*You're* Vance Warner!' she asked and observed at the same time.

'In the flesh.'

Very much so, Caryn agreed. He had foregone his usual blue jeans and Hawaiian print shirt in favor of forest green slacks with a pale green silk shirt, the first few buttons open and revealing a thatch of reddish brown hair on his broad chest.

His glance, tinged with disapproval, flitted over her clothes. She stubbornly determined not to make excuses or explanations about her attire.

She diverted her thoughts from his magnetizing handsomeness. His rudeness in not identifying himself to her was demeaning and infuriating.

'So you like to play little games, Mr Warner?' Caryn taunted with obviously phony lightness as she pulled out her own chair and

18

sat down. 'I can't say I begrudge you your childish play. After all, life on an isolated section of a small island—no movies or television, no public library or even a nearby supermarket—must get quite boring otherwise...' Then her voice became decidedly icy, 'Or perhaps Vance Warner is a name you'd rather not have to identify with.'

His gaze frosted with the chill in her words. 'I had my reasons last night. Reporters from Honolulu have been bothersome since knowledge of the land sale became public. Tourists are always wandering through as if they expect to be greeted by a concession stand and souvenirs.'

'I introduced myself to you last night. You didn't accord me the professional respect of even giving me your name... Well, you said you wanted to be disturbed as little as possible by this project, so you'll pardon me if I eat and run.' Caryn speared her salad with gusto, ignoring her dinner partner.

'I suppose you think I should apologize?'

'Don't you think so?'

'How about a conversational cease-fire?'

She noticed he skirted the delivery of an actual apology, but agreed, 'Fine with me.'

'So what's a nice girl like you doing in a job like this?'

Raising her gaze from her lettuce while she readied a rejoinder, Caryn saw the broad grin indicating he had teasingly baited her. 'Why don't you tell me first how you became lordship of the manorship?'

'A quick tale. I inherited it, and can't take the credit for anything.'

'But it can't be easy to manage such a large operation and hold on to it all.' She had intended a compliment, but realized she'd made a mistake.

His form and features stiffened noticeably, but he said evenly, 'I didn't succeed in holding on to it all. That's why you're here.'

'I didn't mean to sound thoughtless,' Caryn said hastily, recognizing thoughtless was exactly what she'd been. Vance Warner seemed to play havoc with her mind in more ways than one.

'Your turn,' he cued coolly.

'I suppose I inherited my position too, in a way. You've heard of military brats? I was a construction brat. My father was a construction manager for major projects—dams, oil pipelines, power plants, entire towns built by companies for their employees in remote locations. My mother died shortly after I was born, and I lived with my aunt until I was four, while my father tried to get assignments as close as possible to Minnesota and visit often. When I was four, Dad decided I was old enough to come with him—throughout the country, New Orleans to Anchorage and points north. Earlier he'd accepted assignments all over the world; but to give me some semblance of stability and constancy, he limited himself to the United States until I was in college. I must have attended thirty-seven different schools before that, not counting the periods with private tutors for me.'

'You and your father must be very close.'

'We were. When I was a senior in college, he was working on a project in Central America. He was kidnapped by revolutionaries and killed, even though his company paid the ransom demand.' She'd learned to relate her past torment calmly, despite memories of her father still inundating her with a sense of loss.

'That explains how you came by your rather unusual interest in construction management.'

Caryn forced herself to lighter thoughts. 'I earned a college degree in civil engineering, but I'd already learned the business literally from the ground up. My father always let me feel like I was participating. I remember lugging around everything from nails to a couple of bricks when I was a little girl. I'm sure I was a lot more hindrance than help.'

Abruptly, Caryn realized she was revealing more of herself than usual. She'd developed the habit of withholding some of herself from people, even individuals she cared for, as if too much inner sharing was a weapon that might someday pierce her armor of pleasant solitude.

Quickly, she rerouted the conversation into general topics. Vance appeared relieved also to retreat behind a barricade of casual, cocktail

21

party-type dialogue.

Yet despite the armor and the barricades, Caryn had to admit as they progressed to the dessert of pineapple sherbert that she did find Vance Warner exciting, just as he had teasingly warned that afternoon. Or had he been joking? Surely he was aware of his magnetic effect on women, and had guessed that Caryn would be no exception.

But Caryn would be an exception, she steeled her resolve. She wouldn't delude herself that the reciprocal interest she perceived from him could be anything more than her convenient location in an area not populated by many unattached females. And she was probably imagining personal interest on his part anyway.

'Walk you to the cottage,' Vance offered after dessert had been prolonged as much as possible.

'I doubt any dangerous tourists are lurking about, and I'm sure my company hasn't dispatched any more construction superintendents with homicidal Toyotas,' Caryn declined lightly. She forcibly dispelled beckoning images of Vance's powerful form accompanying her along the narrow path, lingering at her cottage door.

I'm as addlepated as a teenager anticipating her first good-night kiss, Caryn scolded herself. This must be an effect of jet lag.

After good-nights murmured with mutual

undertones of reluctance, Caryn returned to her cottage. She washed her peach pantsuit, blouse, and lingerie as best she could, resigned to driving to Kaunakakai to shop for basic clothing and essentials the next afternoon if the airline hadn't found her luggage by then.

As she finished hanging up her soiled clothes, a knock on the door startled her. Improvising, she commandeered a bright yellow sheet from the cabinet.

Clutching the sheet around her, Caryn cracked the door open and saw Vance. 'Just a minute,' she said, actually closing the door in his face while she attempted to fashion a decidedly unique toga/sari/sarong from the sheet, randomly tucked and folded and twisted and knotted.

Dissatisfied with the style, she admitted Vance anyway.

'Mmmm. Fashions by Cannon. Love your new outfit,' Vance quipped. But his eyes contradicted his teasing tone, gilding her with a silver desire. Diverting his gaze, he mumbled, 'I ought to bring in some more firewood.'

He left before Caryn could protest or ask why he'd come in the first place.

Moments later he returned with the promised fuel for a blaze. 'I thought you might take advantage of my absence to slip into something less comfortable.'

Finally, Caryn explained about her lost luggage.

'And I thought you were wearing the same outfit day in and day out as a protest to your femininity, to prove that, like a man, clothes didn't interest you,' he grinned.

'I bet you were planning to haul me into the general store against my will, have the ladies of the town fix me up with a bath and a frilly dress, and have me emerge a glamorous woman with a totally changed personality, capable of popping out men's eyes in awe.'

He chuckled again, a titillating rumble. 'A similar scenario had crossed my mind, except that you've been a glamorous woman all along despite the continuous clothing.'

This time his gaze didn't waver, and Caryn feared the attraction she saw there was reflected in her own eyes. 'Why did you come?' she asked, wary of his response.

'Oh,' he seemed to consciously joggle himself into recollection, then reached into his shirt pocket. 'This diagram must be yours.'

Embarrassed, Caryn remembered. 'I'd planned to work while I ate at the kitchen table. I must have set my paper down there before Hira directed me to the dining room.'

'Yes, I'm sorry to say that's where Hira found it. Until Hira explained, I was hoping you'd left this behind intentionally.'

'To bring you to the cottage?' Caryn was astounded at his first conclusion, even though he recognized he'd been wrong. But she couldn't deny her pleasure at his presence, much as she was trying to ignore the physical and emotional sensations rampaging through her at his nearness. She did manage to clarify, 'I'm not into games, Vance.'

'That's why you were so annoyed with what I considered a playful deception earlier?'

'I suppose so.' She shrugged. 'Maybe I'm just a dull thinker. I see things in terms of mechanics, straight lines, building blocks, squared corners. I can't be bothered with deviations.'

'I'd say you're anything but dull, Caryn Tallis.'

Vance stepped toward her and, mesmerized, Caryn held her ground. His strong hand reached forth, cradling the side of her neck, then tracing around the front of her throat, under her chin, along her cheek. Never had one hand blazed such a path, igniting fires throughout Caryn's body.

His fingers lightly caressed her cheek, glided along her throat, edged the loose, scooped border of the sheet hovering inches above her breasts. Caryn tried to dredge up the determination to stop him if he attempted to breach that flimsy barrier.

But he paused, and his palm moved upward to gently grasp her shoulder.

Involuntarily, her face inclined upward, raising her lips to his at the same time his sensuous mouth descended. His lips attached to hers with a firm tenderness that set every pore of her being aquiver. After a series of kisses guiding her to increased desire, Vance's tongue silently issued an invitation, slipping between her cooperative lips, touching and tasting the tip of her tongue.

He moved to encircle Caryn with his arms, to enfold her to him.

Caryn feared that once she experienced the total power of his form, sensed the full force of his masculinity, she could lose herself to him. Struggling to recover a semblance of her usual control, she stiffened against the gentle leadership of his arms urging her toward him.

'Vance, I'll only be here a few months,' she murmured.

His low sigh reverberated through Caryn's being. 'Yes,' he acknowledged. 'So what are you saying, really?'

'I'm saying there's no point in our getting involved.'

'Must there be a point?'

Caryn's next words were a spoken sigh. 'I don't know, Vance ... I don't know.'

Hesitantly, he receded from her with one last tender stroking of his hand over her hair. 'Good night, Caryn.'

How many more good-nights would she hear from Vance in parting? A few months could seem a lifetime—an interminable lifetime, or a very short lifetime, Caryn now realized.

For half an hour she paced the cottage.

Her choice of career over love and marriage had been carefully considered and decided. She was accustomed to a gypsy existence. She wanted to see the world and watch buildings take shape under her management.

She wanted no commitment. Suddenly she was facing a desire for Vance Warner which threatened to overwhelm her, but she found that she couldn't permit those feelings to grow when commitment was impossible.

Unfamiliar sensations were racing through her body, heedless of her plans for the future.

Men had never posed a problem for her before. Growing up on the construction sites with her father, she'd been like a protected little sister to the workers. When she'd reached the tempting teen years, the other workers had kept tight reins on anyone who had cast more than a brotherly eye in her direction.

In college she'd dated casually, but most of the male students had been more interested in women majoring in home economics than those they perceived to threaten their masculinity and compete for their jobs.

And then there was Ben. Ben, who accepted her on an equal basis and who was now managing the construction of a hotel in Singapore for Resorts Inc. They'd briefly discussed marriage, but decided that wasn't for two transient construction superintendents. He was a good friend still.

Caryn wondered what might have happened

if Ben had aroused the same sensations and emotions that flowed within her in Vance's mere presence.

Maybe it's the wind, she decided. Scientists theorized that winds in some areas affected human behavior.

Why else would she be lying in bed awake for so long, feeling suddenly alone on the king-sized mattress.

CHAPTER THREE

The next morning the sun shone brightly and the wind had quieted to a breeze. Caryn was glad, since her clothing had failed to dry completely in the humid atmosphere.

She'd slept through the six-thirty breakfast hour, but begged a couple of pieces of toast from Hira. Vance didn't appear.

Responding to the tuneless hum of a small aircraft around nine o'clock, Caryn hurried toward the WindsEnd landing strip, which her company had negotiated permission to use. The familiar look of the Cessna was explained when the pilot opened his door.

'Morning, Caryn.'

Caryn was genuinely pleased. 'Mike, hi! I didn't know you were the pilot for this charter.'

'Neither did I two days ago, but it's good to see you again.' Mike O'Riley, tall and lean, unfolded himself from the Cessna. Friendly hazel eyes smiled above a slightly crooked nose as he raked his fingers through his sandy hair.

She peered into the interior of the plane to greet Bob Saito, the Japanese-American architect from Honolulu, who was losing a wrestling match with his briefcase in the confined space.

'I'm afraid the site's super muddy today,' Caryn warned.

'These boots were made for slogging,' Bob assured cheerfully, finally able to thrust one leg out the door. He looked quite different in field clothes than in the conservative business suits worn for their previous meetings in Minneapolis. 'How do you and Mike know each other?' Bob asked as they all walked toward the resort site.

'He's my hero, my knight in a white Cessna,' she replied lightly, 'the man who challenged the winds and won—I think,' she added as a strong gust whirled around them.

Mike expanded to Bob, 'Two nights ago when I had to land Caryn at the Molokai airport, the wind was much worse than usual, even worse than we encountered over the channel this morning.'

'The winds guard Molokai,' Bob said. 'Supposedly, that's why it was known for centuries as the Forgotten Isle or the Lonely Isle, because it was practically impossible for boats to approach here until the winds' power was usurped by modern motors.'

'The other theory is that powerful *kahunas*—Hawaiian priests,' Mike clarified to Caryn, 'resided here and prohibited visitors.'

'Maybe both were true. Perhaps the spirits of the *kahunas* still ride the winds.' Caryn herself was surprised at how serious she sounded, and immediately forced an effort at lightness. 'Today they have to content themselves with tossing around the small aircraft approaching the island. The winds sure seemed determined to prevent my arrival the other night.'

'Of course, Molokai's been redubbed the Friendly Isle in this century,' Mike reassured her.

'By some misinformed bureaucrat at the Chamber of Commerce,' she muttered.

'The wind wouldn't have been so noticeable on a larger commercial aircraft,' Bob pointed out.

Caryn explained why she'd missed all the commercial flights. 'So the main airline arranged a charter to get me to Molokai still that night, overlooking the fact that the whole island closes at 6 P.M. Fortunately, Mike knew where to call a friend of his who manages one of the local car rental agencies. Otherwise I could have been abandoned and had to huddle outside the little airport terminal in the rain all night.'

'I'm glad you made it. I was concerned about

your trying to drive through that storm ... I guess your luggage hasn't caught up with you yet,' Mike said, observing her attire.

'No. I have to drive into town this afternoon to do some shopping.'

'You won't find much selection in Kaunakakai. You might have to allot a day to Honolulu. Guess who'd be delighted to fly you there,' Mike grinned.

When they arrived at the construction site, Bob introduced Caryn to the just arrived assistant superintendent, John Umeshi, who in turn introduced them to the few other workers already on the scene. Mike looked bored as he accompanied them around the site, only half listening to the technical discussions and plans, waiting to fly Bob back to Honolulu.

As they prepared to return after noon, Caryn separated from the men at her cottage. She was looking forward to a big, late lunch in town since she didn't want to go to the main house.

'Wait a minute,' Mike's call summoned her back. 'You're not going to Kaunakakai or anywhere else in this.'

He stood by her rented lime green Toyota, nudging with his shoe at one of the tires. She saw the tire was totally flat.

'No problem. I can change a flat,' Caryn assured him.

Mike broke the news: 'All four are like this, Caryn. All four slashed to ribbons.'

Caryn was stunned. Surely Vance wouldn't take such juvenile revenge for her rejection of him last night. Though Vance was admittedly a fan of childish games. And the few plantation workers she'd encountered had been unfriendly. 'Why ... who would...?'

'Maybe kids,' Bob shrugged off. But he didn't look convinced himself.

Mike glanced at his watch. 'Tell you what. I'll drop you at the airport. There are a couple of cabs. One of them ought to be available to take you into Kaunakakai. Then I'll take Bob on to Honolulu for his afternoon meeting, fly back to Molokai, call my friend Joe and get four new tires, meet you in town, and fly you and the tires back here. I'll even help you change them.' Mike's offer seemed a jumble of Hawaiian syllables.

Caryn liked Mike. He was a nice guy. Of course, her company would pay his usual charter fee, though he hadn't mentioned it.

Half an hour later the winds mildly buffeted the Cessna as they descended at Molokai Airport. Caryn asked as she disembarked, once again a bit nauseous, 'Where and what time shall I meet you in town?'

'It's not that big, Caryn,' Mike chuckled. 'I won't have any trouble finding you in a couple of hours.'

She hadn't even reached the tiny terminal before the plane took off again.

She instructed the cabdriver to take her to

the center of town. With an impish grin he delivered her smack-dab to the middle of the middle block of the three-block-long main street.

Kaunakakai was not at all tropical in appearance. Instead, it resembled a Western movie set, complete with a few false facades. Not the only false facades on Molokai, she mused. Everything seemed in need of a coat of paint or three.

She noted that the windows of grocery stores incongruently displayed clothing—splashily printed muumuus and shirts. Caryn finally opted for a general dry goods-type store, which stocked a plethora of housewares, hardware, and clothing scrunched in its small one-room operation.

Although no other customers were visible, the clerk ignored her as Caryn garnered from the limited selection two sets of undergarments, a couple of pairs of jeans, three shirts. A long dress of blended orange and pink in Hawaiian fashion brightly commanded her gaze. With a silent gesture toward a curtained, telephone booth-sized dressing room, the clerk desultorily acknowledged her request to try it on. Caryn couldn't resist the dress, although she anticipated no occasion to wear it on Molokai.

She decided to wear one set of clean clothes, and relegated her now despised peach pantsuit to a paper sack.

The clerk totaled her purchases and accepted her payment without other comment.

'Is there a drugstore nearby?' Caryn figured her purchases entitled her to ask.

'That way,' was the abbreviated answer as the woman again halfheartedly gestured with her hand.

Caryn picked her way across the street, skirting puddles remaining from the previous days' deluge. The street had neither traffic lights nor much traffic.

'Wait,' a masculine voice ordered.

Great. Now I'll probably get a ticket for jaywalking or something, Caryn speculated. Instead, when she turned, she saw Mike hurrying congenially toward her. 'You're back already?'

'Honolulu's less than half an hour's flight. I borrowed a car from my rental friend, and here I am.'

'Rental friend,' she giggled at his term. 'You know, I think that might be exactly what Molokai needs, a rent-a-friend service. If the charter business ever fails, you might consider it.'

He relieved her of her sack and took her hand in his as they walked along. 'I'm here now, Caryn, and I'm free,' he said gently, genuinely. 'How about some lunch?'

'I was looking forward to food, but the only restaurant I've seen is the Dairy Queen back by the turn.'

'You have to know the secrets of Molokai,' he imitated a 'Twilight Zone' voice. 'Let's take a walk on the boardwalk, and I'll monopolize you.' He referred to Kaunakakai's raised sidewalk, constructed of lumber planks.

'I've heard of places where they roll up the sidewalks at night. Here they must dismantle them and use them for bed boards,' Caryn quipped.

Mike paused when they reached the next-to-the-last block. 'Here we are.'

'Where are we?' Caryn puzzled.

'The eatery I promised you.'

She reconnoitered again. No sign indicated a restaurant, and dark windows of opaque glass guarded against passersby discovering the building's clandestine activity.

'This is the Mid-Nite Inn,' Mike introduced.

'Will it be open this early?'

'Of course. It's certainly not open at midnight,' Mike clarified drolly as he held the door open. A potpourri of cooking smells, not unpleasant, tantalized Caryn's nostrils.

Islanders occupied several booths and tables. Caryn knew it wasn't her imagination that the normal babble of conversation hushed within seconds after they entered, replaced by a few whispered comments. Assorted pairs of eyes watched coldly as Mike selected a table near the center of the room.

The hostility seemed tangible, hovering in the air, surrounding them.

35

'The Dairy Queen at the North Pole would have a warmer reception,' she muttered to Mike.

Perhaps they were reacting to her being an unknown woman, a *haole* at that, invading territory not normally frequented by tourists. Only one other female besides the waitress was in the small restaurant—a stunningly beautiful Asian lady seated alone in a dim far corner. Caryn asked Mike, 'Are the Molokaians like this with all strangers?'

He hesitated before answering. 'No, not as bad as you may be experiencing. You're probably getting unusual treatment.'

In more ways than Mike knew since her arrival on Molokai. 'Why?'

'You must realize that the residents either have remained here or have moved to Molokai because they like the island the way it is, the last frontier of the true Hawaii. They don't want real estate developments and hordes of tourists. They fear Molokai becoming like the other islands. You wouldn't believe how much even Maui has changed in the last five or six years. To be honest, that's probably why your tires were slashed. It's not the first time that's happened, even to one-day tourists.'

'So I'm their scapegoat.' Caryn was nonetheless relieved to no longer harbor even the slightest suspicion that Vance might have been the vandal.

'You do represent the new resort

development—'

'Which is going to provide employment as well as attracting additional dollars to the economy.'

'They don't want that as much as they want to be left alone, even though plenty of Molokaians need jobs right now.'

Scattered customers called out and waved convivial greetings to a newcomer. Glancing over her shoulder, Caryn saw that the recipient of all this welcome was none other than Vance Warner.

She turned back to face Mike, determined to continue their conversation as Vance shook hands and returned remarks while he made his way across the room. When he paused to chat with a man at the next table, Caryn found herself unwillingly admiring the strong profile of his body and the chiseled features of his face.

He turned, and a tease tugged the corners of his mouth as he alluded to her wish for a businesslike relationship between them. 'Good afternoon, Ms. Tallis.' The 'Ms.' was deliberately drawn out, the *z* sound vibrating on the tip of his tongue.

A tongue that Caryn recently had enjoyed, she remembered with dismay. She acknowledged with a slight smile, 'Mr Warner.'

Mike rose and extended his hand. 'Mike O'Riley, Mr Warner. We've met before. I run a flight-charter service out of Honolulu.'

Caryn realized Mike had to be on the constant lookout for business. Dozens of young charter pilots scrambled for a living among the islands.

'Maybe we can chat about flying sometime.' Vance's tone didn't match the congeniality of his statement. 'I fly my own Beechcraft.'

'I noticed the hangar when I landed at WindsEnd this morning.'

'Please excuse me,' Vance said. 'I'm meeting someone.' He continued to kid Caryn with his formal politeness. 'I'll see you at dinner one of these nights, Ms.'—again the last letter seesawed up and down before he released it—'Tallis.'

Vance's someone proved to be the beautiful woman Caryn had noticed at the corner table. She rose as he approached, leaning halfway over the table and displaying a fetching décolleté. She ran a delicate hand along his cheek as they kissed lightly, then laughed at something he said.

Abruptly, Caryn realized that Vance's formality may not have been in jest, but a serious act performed for this woman or the other customers in the restaurant, so they wouldn't be aware that Vance had been more than amicable to her just last night.

Caryn wished she and Mike could leave, wished at least she was seated where the affectionate couple in the corner weren't in her direct line of vision. But she wouldn't give

Vance the satisfaction of moving.

She did have a pressing question to ask Mike. 'Why are people so friendly to him, when they're so cold to me? Neither I nor anyone like me would be here if he hadn't sold the land in the first place. Or are they hypocritical, pretending to like him because he has influence?'

'Could be. Or maybe they understand that he was forced to sell off that chunk of real estate.'

'Forced? If you mean my employer threatened or strong-armed Warner—'

'No. But inflation, and recession, and the economic fact that pineapple now can be grown less expensively in other countries probably muscled in. That's another reason the population's a little uptight; a lot of pineapple workers on Molokai have been laid off, not only by WindsEnd but by other growers. Warner may have had a cash-flow problem. I've heard that he tried to keep his oldest employees on as long as possible, even retrained some as *paniolos*—that's the Hawaiian word for "cowboys." '

Caryn remembered a clause in the sales contract for which she previously hadn't recognized the significance. 'The agreement does state that the construction project must employ former WindsEnd workers first, and other permanent residents of Molokai second, for any positions they're qualified to fill, rather than importing other workers.'

Softening toward Vance, she reminded herself that one humanitarian gesture, which actually cost him nothing personally, did not alter their situation.

Caryn tried to concentrate on Mike. Seldom had she gazed with such total raptness at any man, appearing to hang on his every word. As Vance was being entertained by another companion, so would she be.

But more frequently than she liked, her glance darted to the corner. On one of those occasions she saw Vance looking toward their table while his companion chatted gaily. Caryn quickly averted her eyes.

She learned that Mike had been a helicopter pilot in Vietnam and that he'd had offers of jobs with commercial airlines, even flown with one for a while. But now his goal was to operate a successful but laid-back island charter company.

Lunch was roast beef, gravy, potatoes, and salad—satisfactory but not an epicurean delight. Caryn chided herself for classifying Mike as meat and potatoes and Vance as something more exotic. But then meat and potatoes were solid, generally held no unpleasant surprises, and were much more necessary to one's healthy existence.

'We've been talking all about me, nothing about you,' Mike interrupted himself.

Caryn repeated the same background

information she'd related to Vance last night, yet oddly didn't feel as wary of revealing herself to Mike. So she added further details.

'My boss, Jordan Nash, established and heads up the conglomerate developing the resort here on Molokai, as well as several others around the world. He and my father were friends from the time they served together as young men in the Navy Seabees, the Mobile Construction Battalion.'

She continued: 'I've worked for Jordan since I graduated, but this is the first big project I've handled on my own. In fact, I put up something of a fight to get this assignment. The company wanted to shuffle me off to Singapore to supervise just the last phase of a hotel being built there, so I feel I have to prove myself.'

She didn't explain to Mike that she'd won this project away from Ben, the one man who'd come close to being her lover or even her husband.

Until Vance.

She was stunned at that thought crossing her mind. What was the matter with her anyway?

Competing for the same assignment hadn't even been one of the problems she and Ben had considered when they'd agreed marriage wasn't feasible for the two of them.

Caryn deliberately raised her voice slightly from its previous intimate level. 'The resort at WindsEnd is designed to blend with the environment. Two buildings, three stories each, will have a total of sixty condominium apartments for rental to tourists whenever the owners aren't occupying them, which is most of the year. Another three-story building will house sixty motel rooms as well as the clubhouse and offices.'

She noted with satisfaction that much of the conversation at surrounding tables had halted as the other diners tried to overhear what she was saying. 'The two condo buildings will sit in a V shape, facing away from each other toward the ocean, with open space between. The third building, set further back, also will have an ocean view through the open space. There will be tennis courts, a swimming pool, shuffleboard, Ping-Pong, the usual amenities. And a putting green.' Jordan Nash had wanted to add an entire eighteen-hole golf course, and was still hoping to persuade Vance to sell more land.

Perceiving the purpose of Caryn's slightly louder voice, Mike pitched in. 'Sounds wonderful. It'll be great for the charter business, great for all the businesses on Molokai.'

'And provide many jobs, both during and after construction,' Caryn added, although she knew she was repeating herself to Mike.

Their not too subtle pep talk was interrupted by Mike's beeper, hung on his belt. 'That's my answering service in Honolulu trying to reach me.' He excused himself, hurrying to the pay

42

telephone at the back.

Caryn had to remind herself that, though Honolulu was on the entirely separate island of Oahu, it wasn't far away. She toyed with her Coke while Mike completed his call, looking very happy. Then to her surprise, Mike stopped at Vance's table and exchanged conversation with him.

'Caryn, come on back here a minute,' Mike summoned.

Caryn managed to approach Vance's table with a poise belying the turmoil of her feelings. She certainly hadn't intended to interrupt his rendezvous with his current conquest.

Mike explained, 'I'm sorry to desert you, but a couple in Honolulu will charter my plane for at least three full days provided I'm back in Honolulu within the hour. Vance drove his van to town, so there'll be plenty of room for you and all your tires to ride back to WindsEnd with him.'

A splinter of distress lodged in Caryn's mind. She'd determined that the best way to avoid involvement with Vance Warner was to see as little of him as possible. Now she'd have a two-hour ride in Vance's company. And he probably wasn't thrilled to have her forced on him, when he obviously had made other plans. Caryn feigned calmness. 'I don't want to impose. I'll just rent another car.'

'And pay for two rental cars at the same time? If your company has money to throw away, many worthy community projects could use it,' Vance stated with irrefutable logic. 'I'm driving to WindsEnd anyway, but my business won't be completed for a couple of hours.'

At least a couple of hours, Caryn thought cattily as she glanced at Vance's gorgeous 'business,' to whom he was introducing her at that moment.

'Caryn Tallis, Tami Nakamura. Tami's a stewardess with TransGlobal, flies all over the world.'

'But returns to Molokai every chance she gets,' Tami commented softly, her dark eyes flowing toward Vance with affection. Tami turned her attention to Caryn. 'It's so nice to meet you, Caryn,' she said with seeming sincerity. 'I understand you've got a tough job ahead of you. I hope we can get together now and then when I'm at WindsEnd. You may become lonely for some good old-fashioned girl talk.'

Caryn couldn't ward off a nebulous reaction. Here was a woman she wanted to dislike, even though she had no reason except juvenile jealousy over a man whom she'd already planned to avoid. Yet Tami was the only person who'd been friendly to her on the whole of Molokai. Except Vance, whose motives she suspected might be born of convenience. Caryn figured Mike couldn't be counted, since their acquaintance had started in Honolulu.

'I'll look forward to that,' Caryn said, uncertain of the truth of her reply. Somehow Caryn didn't want to know that Tami visited WindsEnd regularly.

Then anger on behalf of both she and Tami erupted within Caryn. Anger stirred by Vance Warner. Tami obviously didn't know that Vance had made advances toward Caryn last night. Well, she'd show Vance Warner that not every woman was pliant as clay in his presence, by riding back to WindsEnd displaying the same lack of interest in him that she'd have in any faceless bus driver.

Caryn said formally, 'A couple of hours will be fine. I haven't finished my shopping yet anyway. Where shall I meet you?'

Before he left, Mike transferred the four tires from his borrowed car to Vance's van, along with Caryn's prior purchases.

She continued the shopping she'd planned to facilitate avoiding Vance if she felt a desire to do otherwise. Not *if* but *when*—she reminded herself, for she was too intelligent not to recognize his magnetic attraction. And since meeting Tami, she was more determined than ever not to be tempted into a fleeting affair with Vance just because he became a little lonely whenever Tami was away.

At various stores she acquired a two-burner hot plate, a couple of pans, a can opener, settings of plastic dinnerware and silverware, and other rudimentary utensils. She would not have to eat every meal at the main house if she deemed it hazardous to her mental and emotional health to do so.

Caryn's impression of Kaunakakai was that everything seemed scaled down, even the people and the cars and the dogs. She felt like Ms. Gulliver plunked down in the middle of Lilliput.

That image was perpetuated by the grocery store, where the carts were miniatures of the standard, but nonetheless difficult to maneuver past each other in unusually narrow aisles.

Cultures contrasted and coexisted in the market. Taro chips vied with potato chips. Instead of canned tuna, Caryn could have selected canned boiled octopus or cellophane bags of sardines or hot red cuttlefish legs. Other exotica such as shredded mango, sweet-and-sour plums, and *li hing mui* also were available in cellophane bags.

Caryn gathered up three sacks full of groceries, passing up the hot red cuttlefish legs. Mostly, she bought snackable items, or meals in a single, easy-to-heat can.

She returned to the appointed meeting place at the 'center of the city' half an hour early, but Vance was already waiting.

Loading her sacks into the back of his van, he asked, 'Don't you like Hira's cooking?'

'It's delicious.' Caryn offered no explanation.

But Vance insisted on one. 'Then why are you doing this?'

'As the project gets going, I won't always be able to stick to a definite schedule for meals.' The statement was true, even though it hadn't been her prime motivation for stocking such a large supply of groceries. 'This way I won't have to worry about it. I'll let Hira know in advance when I won't be eating at your house, so she won't prepare too much food.'

Vance's cloudy eyes seemed unaccepting of her rationale. But he didn't protest.

As they turned onto the highway, Caryn was only too aware of Vance's proximity less than an arm's length away. Her wary glance took in the tantalizing ripple of muscles beneath faded denim stretched across his thighs.

Though recognizing her next remark as unworthily childish and nettling, she said it anyway, as if subconsciously intending to add another brick to the barrier between them. 'Sorry to trouble you for the ride. I hope you didn't have to cut your afternoon short on my account. You did tell me originally that Vance Warner wanted to be disturbed as little as possible by the Resorts Inc. project.'

Caryn studiously stared straight ahead through the windshield, yet the periphery of her vision noted a tightening of his chiseled jaw.

'You've already disturbed me quite a lot.'

'I'm not the one who requested this ride.'

47

'You know very well that's not what I mean.'

Usually cool, collected Caryn couldn't believe that she was the one speaking. 'I'm sure Tami soothed any disturbances.'

'Time with Tami is always pleasant,' he confirmed smoothly.

Silence intruded between them, hovering like a chill fog, for nearly half an hour.

'Oh, wait, can we stop here?' Caryn forgot her annoyance with both herself and Vance in her enthusiasm at encountering one friend she'd forgotten. A small white church had shone like a beacon through the coal black night when she'd first driven this route. Though Caryn wasn't a particularly religious person, the gleaming white symbol had beamed a message of encouragement and hope to her when she was disheartened, exhausted, and a little frightened by the storm.

Vance looked surprised at her interest, but swerved right and stopped in front. 'This is one of many small churches built on Molokai by Father Damien,' he explained. 'He was a Belgian priest who was the first to really aid the lepers banished to the peninsula on the other side of the island in the late 1800s. He eventually contracted the disease himself.'

Perhaps the church in a small way continued to help individuals banished and unwelcome on Molokai. 'I'm familiar with the story. In fact, I want to visit Kalaupapa before I leave Molokai.' Belatedly realizing that sounded like a hint for Vance to escort her, she quickly added, 'I'll ask Mike to fly me down to the peninsula sometime.'

Caryn read the plaque outside the church, which was constructed in New England rather than Hawaiian style. She mentally bade it a fond farewell as they drove away.

That brief interlude had softened the atmosphere between them. Vance transformed into a knowledgeable but impersonal guide, commentating on the sights and history of Hawaii in general and Molokai in particular.

A few miles past the church the highway began taking turns with itself as to which side of the pavement had its holes mostly patched. Zigzags of smooth road alternated with lengths pocked with gaping, jarring holes of varying sizes, like a jigsaw puzzle with lots of pieces missing.

Some time later they passed a highway repair truck, with two men filling one minicrater from shovels. Adapting rapidly to her surroundings, Caryn somehow wasn't surprised that none of the other holes ahead of or behind the repair truck were patched.

Even the shoreline politely took turns with itself. Slim expanses of pale sand separated strips of jumbled ebony boulders fronting the ocean—again and again—a necklace of seemingly evenly spaced but contrasting sections beaded around the slender throat of Molokai.

Vance pointed out the fishponds they passed. Small pools of ocean by the shore were dammed off by black lava stones. 'The Hawaiians captured and maintained fish there for the *alii*, their royalty, much as we'd keep cattle on a feedlot.'

When no new material for his travelogue presented itself in the next minutes, Vance gestured toward the postcards protruding from the outside pocket of Caryn's purse. 'It looks like you plan to keep in touch with several friends.'

'Yes.' Only her aunt and three others.

A pause ensued before Vance's next question, in a slightly constricted tone. 'Will one or more of those cards be going to a male friend?'

Caryn suppressed the obvious response that it was none of his business, instead replying honestly but without elaboration, 'Yes.' Maybe if Vance assumed her to be otherwise attached, he wouldn't try to pursue anything more than a casual acquaintance between them.

Let him think she had someone important to her, as he had Tami. She continued to stay in touch with Ben in Singapore, with whom she'd remained friends after their romance had ended.

If her relationship with Ben could be termed a romance in the ultimate sense of the word, Caryn now realized. Her feelings for Vance seemed so strong after only two days that she genuinely feared the intense course her emotions might follow if allowed to run free. While she and Ben had thought themselves in love, Caryn now wondered to what supreme heights that simple word might propel her if ever shared with Vance.

Vance maintained a passive expression. After a brief pause he took a more general direction in their conversation, asking lightly, 'What will you tell your friends about Molokai?'

Caryn replied without hesitation. 'I'll say Molokai is a paradox paradise.' She cited the contrasting shoreline. The half-smooth, half-holey road. Grocery stores selling clothing and hardware stores selling food. The tiny churches of different religions holding forth side by side on the eastern approach to Kaunakakai. The Mid-Nite Inn that closed early. The perpetual wreath of gray clouds hanging about the hilltops while the sun shone brightly along the shore.

An island designated 'Lonely' in the last century and, inaccurately, 'Friendly' now.

She stopped short of referring to another paradox, Vance Warner himself, born of Molokai. A man at times seeming tough and rude, at other times hinting at a capacity for tenderness and caring. A man who last night seemed interested in Caryn, but actually was involved with the beautiful, congenial Tami. A man who sometimes seemed to want to reach to Caryn in a realm surpassing the physical, but who hastened to withdraw within himself lest that occur.

As did she, Caryn realized abruptly. Molokai had produced a new paradox in the body and soul of Caryn Tallis. A woman who wanted to know Vance Warner better, but panicked at the prospect of involvement. Who wanted to be involved, but feared the pain of imminent parting. A woman who'd chosen an interesting career that could take her all over the world with no prospect of becoming bored with a particular place, but who already was beginning to regret her ultimate departure from a tiny island where the residents and the elements had been mostly hostile.

A modern woman experiencing normal sensuality, but having difficulty reconciling those needs in actual practice when she knew she'd never want marriage. Marriage was out of the question in view of the constant temporary assignments and relocation of her career.

Paradoxes that added up to hell, not paradise.

In a flash of insight, Caryn wondered whether she and Vance were slotted in the same category. Two people satisfied with their lifestyles. Two loners who'd always been happy independent and alone, and who would steadfastly beat back any threat to their comfortable state.

They were nearing the main entrance to WindsEnd, Caryn recognized, when she saw herds of cattle grazing in fenced pastures.

The trees along this stretch of land had been sculpted autocratically by the winds. Their branches grew only *mauka*, away from the sea—as if pruned and disciplined by a stern gardener. Caryn mused that the *paniolos* must periodically rotate the cows to prevent them from becoming lean on one side and fat on the other.

Perhaps those same winds had sculpted Vance Warner into the person he was now— one-sided, single-minded, yet strong for having survived their onslaught. Standing solitary in the wind.

And how would the winds of Molokai shape Caryn Tallis? Not at all, she determined. She would leave Molokai exactly as she'd arrived, with no mental or emotional encumbrances nor regrets.

CHAPTER FOUR

As the clouds often blotted out the sun, so had Caryn succeeded in avoiding Vance much of the time. They had enjoyed dinner together a few times at the main house. But Caryn always excused herself early and declined Vance's offers to walk her back to the cottage.

Warming water on her hot plate for her fourth morning of instant oatmeal and instant coffee, Caryn vowed to buy a toaster the next time she went into town. That was probably the closest she'd come to gourmet cooking in her cottage.

The construction crew had started clearing the land for the resort, working around patches of reprieved palms and shrubbery.

Caryn tried to shake the morose mood descending on her as she viewed the site from a vantage point, wearing a hooded yellow slicker against the rain drizzling down again that morning.

She couldn't help thinking that the raw red earth bled from its wounds, and the sky wept.

Head bowed against the downpour as she strode along the periphery of the site, Caryn bumped into a strong shoulder. 'Oh, sorry.' Looking up, she saw, in a mixture of horror and delight, that the shoulder belonged to Vance.

'You seem determined to run into me whenever it rains, with or without a car,' Vance commented bemusedly, but seemed distracted as he resumed his gaze across the defaced land.

Her own eyes followed his for moments, in silence, and she felt irrationally guilty at causing him pain. 'It won't look so bad once the buildings are up, and the complex will be beautiful when the landscaping is finished,' she comforted ineffectually.

'I know,' he replied softly and without malice, 'but it won't be the same, and it won't be mine.'

Caryn had to exercise all her self-control to refrain from reaching out to Vance, from wrapping her arms around him tightly, from pressing her body against his for whatever consolation she might offer. Instead, she forced casual conversation: 'The work crew will gradually expand over the next couple of weeks. Others are arriving today.'

'The more, the merrier,' Vance said slowly in a measured tone. 'And the sooner you'll all be gone.' His silver eyes seemed to drill to the depths of her soul.

'Yes,' she confirmed without outward emotion.

'Is there anything you need that you haven't been able to get here?'

Oh yes, yes, most definitely yes, Caryn's mind fluttered as she stared back at him.

'I'll be flying to Honolulu in a few days. Do you want me to bring you anything?' he repeated.

She recovered momentarily. 'Thank you, but I've already arranged to charter Mike's plane on Tuesday. The airline never has found my luggage, so I have to do a little shopping before we get even busier here.'

Vance jammed his hands into his jeans pockets as if to confine them from touching her. 'You could fly over and back with me,' he offered with the same feigned nonchalance permeating their conversation.

We'd crash into the sea if I couldn't keep my hands off you, the way I'm feeling now, Caryn thought. But she replied politely, 'Thank you, but I've already reserved Mike for the day. It wouldn't be right to cancel on such a short notice, in case he's missed other customers.'

'Whatever you say,' Vance shrugged. Then he said in parting, 'I've got to get back.'

Caryn met the other workers who arrived that afternoon, except for Kano, the general foreman, who was otherwise occupied when the assistant superintendent, John Umeshi, introduced her around.

John already had made his attitude about having a female boss quite clear, with a mixture of put-downs and come-ons. Caryn had responded firmly to John, though she disliked having to show him who was boss. Now the increasing subtlety of his remarks made rejoinders more difficult without sounding petty and belligerent herself.

Friday night Caryn ate crackers and soup in front of her unlit fireplace, trying to convince herself that thoughts of Vance Warner intruded at the most inopportune times only because she associated him with a full, square meal.

Saturday Caryn went in search of a Vanceless dinner, reversing the route they'd driven previously as she set out to explore the island. Niggling at her mind was the awareness that she sought anything that might divert her thoughts from Vance.

By midafternoon Caryn stood at the pinnacle of the high cliff, or *pali,* which surrounded and severed from the rest of the island the eternal shame of all Hawaii. Waves and time had erased from the now placid beach far below all signs of the torment which once rendered the name Molokai not only Lonely, but synonymous with hell.

Beginning in 1866, lepers had been quarantined on that isolated jut of land. Some drowned before reaching it, pushed overboard from the transport ships that refused to come all the way in to shore. The survivors were abandoned with no food, no shelter, no medical treatment, no organization except the tyranny of the strong over the weak, and no hope until the arrival in 1873 of the dedicated Belgian priest Father Damien.

Today the sky was unfriendly as usual. Swarthy, aggressive clouds maundered about, already seizing the tops of some distant hills, threatening to envelope this one soon.

Yet despite the mottle of the day, a stream of sunlight beamed through upon the current settlement of Kalaupapa on the peninsula, as if to reverse in this century the malevolence of the last. The small village gleamed white, with flowers blooming beside well-maintained

57

houses on neatly laid out streets. Those who remained there today did so by choice, since treatment had been discovered for Hansen's disease, as leprosy was now called.

Caryn vowed to join sometime the mule train tour that wound its way along the ancient, narrow trail down the *pali* to the village.

She wondered glumly whether she'd been drawn to this particular place because of the feeling of ostracism she'd been experiencing during her own stay on Molokai.

Then, determined to play tourist, she strode along the path strewn with pine needles to the Phallic Rock. At this six-foot-high, somewhat anatomically shaped, unrolling stone, the ancient Hawaiians had left offerings and prayed for fertility. Caryn didn't spend much time there.

She glanced quickly at nearby petroglyphs before returning to her car and retracing her route between pineapple fields, along the asphalt ribbon tying the *pali* to the main Highway 45.

She stopped at an enormous grove of coconut palms that seemed the ultimate tropicana. The breezes propelled high fronds stretching toward the sky like fans of gods.

She was anticipating a leisurely and tranquilizing stroll among the majestic palms to the far beach when she noticed the signs warning of Danger from Falling Coconuts.

Even this beautiful place was inhospitable toward Caryn Tallis! And the way things were going, she'd surely get bonked on the head if she took her chances!

Disappointed, Caryn contained herself to a brief walk along the outer edge, and read the explanatory sign identifying the ten-acre Kapuaiwa Grove, with one thousand coconut palms planted by King Kamehameha V in the 1860s.

She replenished her supply of groceries in Kaunakakai, and bought a toaster.

Around six o'clock she went to the Hotel Molokai. The hotel's restaurant was one of two fine dining places on the island, she'd learned, the other being at the Sheraton at the far west end.

She passed a small fountain constructed of black lava rock, with a sign indicating it had been appropriately blessed by a *kahuna* so that the volcano goddess, Pele, wouldn't be angered that the material had been relocated. Caryn began to picture a grand man-made waterfall for her own resort.

She'd ordered batter-fried shrimp and was in the process of decimating the salad bar when she heard from behind her, '*Aloha*, Miss Tallis.'

She turned to see a mountain of a man with hair white as snow atop his bronze-colored body. He continued, 'I am Kano I am 100 percent Hawaiian,' as if it were all part of his

59

name.

He looked familiar, but...

'I work for you, but I just arrived yesterday. We haven't been introduced.'

'Oh yes, I remember. You're the general foreman.'

They chatted for a few minutes. Caryn was astonished when he asked if he could join her for dinner. A friendly Molokaian!

Kano was, to put it simply, a huge man—the epitome of the true Hawaiians about whom Caryn had read. One of the last bastions of a disappearing race, since the ebullient Hawaiians had long intermarried with all the other ethnic groups comprising the delightful potpourri of Hawaii. Only a small percentage of the islands' population remained true Hawaiian.

'Do you have any children?' Caryn asked midway through dinner.

'Not really. I once married a divorced woman who had a child, but eventually she chose to become a twice-divorced woman, and I haven't seen either of them since, by their choice.'

Caryn was saddened at his statement, because it not only marked an unhappy episode in his own life, but meant he was one more Hawaiian who would be the last of his line.

Kano continued. 'Even though my ex-wife was a Mainlander, she'd lived on Oahu for some time, so I thought she could adjust to Molokai. I was wrong. She returned to Honolulu after a few years. Not many women choose to stay here unless they were born here, and some not even then.'

'I'm sorry,' Caryn said genuinely.

'It couldn't be helped.' He shrugged. 'But then she wasn't my first love, nor my best.' Then realizing he was revealing perhaps too much to a near stranger, albeit a good listener, he veered to a different chapter in his verbal autobiography. 'Let me tell you how I was the star of the University of Hawaii football team until I was interrupted practically mid-touchdown on December 7, 1941.'

'Pearl Harbor,' Caryn confirmed her knowledge of the ignominious start of World War II, or at least America's sudden direct involvement in it.

She thoroughly enjoyed her dinner conversation with Kano. She learned that he'd been a maintenance superintendent for water facilities and systems, employed by the state of Hawaii, before accepting the position with the Resorts Inc. project.

'You gave up a good steady job with the state to take a short-term job with us?' Caryn expressed surprise before realizing that she shouldn't be discouraging competent employees, nor prying into private matters. 'I guess we're paying more,' she said, fumbling.

'Yes, but as you said, yours is hardly a secure

61

job. However, I was able to take an early retirement with the state, and I had other reasons.'

Kano also proved the catalyst for a variety of other people dropping by their table—including a group of *paniolos* from neighboring Maui who had come to Molokai for a rodeo.

The dinner entertainment for the restaurant and adjoining open lounge had been provided by a trio of very young women—not slickly professional, but competent and pleasant. Continuing to accompany themselves on ukelele and guitar, they swung into a rendition of a local favorite, 'Goin' Back to Paniolo Country,' generating broad smiles and participation from many of the customers.

Caryn was more caught up personally in their next number, 'I'll Remember You.' The song had long been one of her favorites, but seemed especially fitting at this time, in this place. The poignant lyrics floating on the haunting Hawaiian lilt of the tune conveyed her thoughts and emotions far beyond the room.

She'd remember Vance. That she already knew. Perhaps that should be enough. Maybe she should just accept the good times for now, accept them as fleeting and destined only to become a memory.

Yet she knew too that the further their relationship progressed, the more indelible the memory would become. Already Vance

Warner had supplanted in her consciousness every other man she'd ever met, even Ben, despite the fact that she and Vance hadn't spent all that much time together.

Caryn certainly didn't want to become one of those dotty little old ladies who populated English literature, with dusty memorabilia and dusty dreams of a man who could be matched by no other. In her heart Caryn recognized that Vance Warner was exactly that kind of man. She briefly pictured herself sitting in a squeaky rocking chair, wearing a flour-sack dress, and clutching a worn snapshot of a towering man with burnished hair and silver eyes.

I'll Remember You...

'Caryn,' Kano's voice prodded. When she finally reacted, he added, 'You were a million miles away.'

No, less than twenty miles away, she lamented to herself as Kano continued, 'I asked if you had plans for Melveen Leed's show tonight.'

'I saw the posters in town.' Melveen Leed Returns, they'd proclaimed. 'But when I inquired, the tickets were sold out.'

'Nonsense. I'm a Molokaian. I can get all the tickets I want,' Kano asserted proudly. 'You want to come?'

'Sure, but am I dressed all right?' Caryn glanced worriedly at her attire of blue jeans and flowered blouse.

'No problem. You'll see all degrees, from

63

very formal to very casual, at the show.'

Later as they joined the crowd surging into the Pau Hana Inn, Kano explained, 'We're very proud of Melveen. She played the part of Sally on "Hawaii Five-0" and appears regularly in hotel shows in Honolulu. She was the first singer from the islands ever to entertain at the Grand Ole Opry in Nashville. Her parents still live on Molokai, though they're divorced.'

Sounds like divorce has replaced bowling as Molokai's favorite indoor pastime, Caryn thought to herself.

After they were seated, Kano chuckled at Caryn's curious study of the waitresses. 'Notice anything different about them?'

'Well, they seem...'

'You got it. Female impersonators.' He lowered his voice and said gruffly, 'I wish they'd throw them all off the island.'

'Now, Kano, that's not exactly the famous *aloha* spirit,' Caryn chided teasingly, and he grinned again.

Melveen Leed's show was fabulous, as her voice and the music of her accompanying combo resounded from beneath a prolific lighted banyan tree in the sizable, semiopen lounge of the Pau Hana. She peppered her show with anecdotes and jokes obviously tailored for the local audience, and enthusiastically made it clear to everyone that she was crazy in love with her doctor-husband.

Caryn was glad the rain had relented for a change and permitted the show to proceed. Yet she was very annoyed with herself for finding something in almost every lyric to relate to her thoughts of Vance.

They were mingling with the crowd afterward when Caryn noticed Kano staring fixedly at something, or someone. Following his gaze, she saw Vance, along with Tami and Hira. A second later Vance turned in their direction. Caryn embarrassedly averted her eyes, knowing he must think she'd been staring at him. When she raised them again, Vance was still looking at her.

Kano distractedly grasped her fingertips to guide her along with him as he forced his way toward the trio.

Caryn and Vance maintained intermittent eye contact, mumbling perfunctory hellos. Vance's coloring and physique were complimented by a short-sleeved raw silk shirt of palest blue, which slicked over his muscular chest and tapered into matching tailored slacks at his firm waistline.

When Caryn turned away, she noticed that Kano and Hira seemed visually melded, engrossed in each other, yet self-conscious and awkward. Hira was very pretty tonight, with her hair styled soft around her face rather than pulled back into its usual strict bun, and her petite figure adorned in a muted island print of violets and blues.

65

Tami was sheathed in a knockout red brocade Chinese-style *cheong-sam*, provocatively slit midway up her slender thigh. Caryn wished she'd planned in advance for this evening so Vance, for once, could have seen her in an attractive, feminine dress.

Tami glanced back and forth between the two couples as if at a tennis match, not sure on which pair to focus, sensing something in the air all around.

'*Aloha*, Hira,' Kano said finally, offering his hand.

'*Aloha*, Kano.' Slowly, shyly, Hira extended her own small hand into his. Kano enclosed it.

'You are beautiful as always, but tonight you have no hibiscus in your hair.'

'No, not since...' Gradually withdrawing her hand, Hira cast her eyes down and blushed.

'Can we get a drink and talk for a while alone, Hira? The others won't mind waiting. We have many years to catch up on.'

The other three all bestowed their unrequired permission with comments of 'Sure, go ahead' and 'We don't mind.'

'Alone? I don't ... There's such a crowd, there's no place...' Hira apparently wanted to spend some time with Kano, yet was hesitant.

'Then let me drive you home. Caryn has her own car. I go to WindsEnd now too.'

'I knew you were working there, but...'

'I live in the modular housing set up temporarily for the employees.'

Again the other three mumbled their approval. Finally, Hira nodded her head in assent.

'Caryn's car is still down the road at the Hotel Molokai. Maybe we can all three have a drink there before we start home,' Kano said.

Vance offered, 'I can drop Caryn.'

You already did, she felt like saying. Clearly, she'd be a fifth wheel for either car, most suitably consigned to the trunk, since both couples wanted to be alone.

Caryn couldn't help thinking as Kano and Hira walked away what an incongruent pair they were—enormous, ebullient Kano and petite, uncommunicative Hira. Yet in all-encompassing Hawaii, they didn't really seem out of place.

Tami excused herself to speak to some friends she spotted, momentarily leaving Caryn and Vance alone.

'I see you go for older men,' Vance teased.

'Older men have a certain savoir-faire.'

'Too bad you couldn't hold on to that one.'

'The competition was too tough.'

Vance reached out and placed his hand lightly on her arm, and she thought surely the crowd could hear her skin sizzle. 'You might have to settle for a younger man someday.'

Tami returned, and the three proceeded to the van, where their seating arrangement had Tami appropriately wedged between Caryn and Vance. Caryn was glad the Hotel Molokai

67

parking lot was less than a mile away.

Tami remained as congenial as on their previous meeting. 'I'll be leaving WindsEnd in the morning, but I'll be visiting again soon,' Tami said to Caryn. 'We can get together for some girl-type chatter then.'

Tami was certainly forthright about her relationship with Vance, leaving Caryn both irrationally jealous and highly sympathetic toward Tami, who obviously didn't know that Vance seemed open to an affair with Caryn too.

While she had no reason to dislike Tami, she couldn't cope with becoming her close pal either. She managed an amicable but abbreviated 'Maybe so.'

Tami continued convivially, 'I spend at least a couple of days a month at WindsEnd. We'll probably see each other at dinner some night.'

'Yes. I eat dinner at the main house occasionally.' After all, it's in the contract. Let Bluebeard worry for a while whether she was going to reveal his attempted philandering to his mistress.

After Caryn was delivered back to the Hotel Molokai, their two separate vehicles joined the caravan returning east on Highway 45. As the distance increased, the traffic thinned.

Once again Caryn felt the eyestrain of driving through blackest night, though this time she could focus on a pair of red taillights, which she was sure belonged to Vance's van.

The red minibeacons zagged back and forth as he steered around the long-lost portions of the highway. Caryn wondered if experience made one more successful at avoiding hazards.

It seemed she'd always be bringing up the rear, following behind Tami and gosh knows how many other women.

CHAPTER FIVE

On Sunday, the sun enjoyed its namesake day, scampering around the sky and skirting the constant clouds that encircled the hilltops.

Caryn felt as unsubstantive and migratory as those billowy ashen puffs drifting on the whim of the breeze. As the clouds dodged the sun, so must she evade any contact with Vance, whose burning touch could evaporate her.

Caryn supposed she should try one of the beaches today, but couldn't generate any enthusiasm. She couldn't stay in her cottage avoiding Vance every weekend, yet no activity seemed appealing without him.

She responded to a tapping on the door with eagerness mingled with anxiety. As she had both hoped and dreaded, Vance stood before her. His own print shirt that day was predominantly royal blue, setting off the silver in his eyes.

'I see you've adopted my fashion style,' he

kidded, referring to her jeans and bright orange Hawaiian print shirt. 'Nice outfit, but I think I liked the sheet better.'

Caryn smiled self-consciously.

Vance said, 'I assume even big bosses take Sundays off. Join me for breakfast, then I'll show you around the plantation. You do ride?'

'You mean something besides Toyotas?'

'Funny you should mention that. I have a fine mare named Toyota... You'll find that creatures on Molokai can be gentle.'

'It's been some time since I've been aboard a horse,' Caryn stalled. But her vocal cords began to operate independently of her brain. 'Okay, that sounds like fun.'

They consumed an enormous breakfast, then Vance packed a saddlebag with a picnic lunch prepared by Hira.

Vance's palms as he helped Caryn mount her strawberry roan seemed to ignite Caryn's skin. His hands lingered at her waist longer than necessary before he moved to his own regal palomino.

Vance guided her around the plantation. Rectangular-shaped pineapple fields were laid out diagonally to each other, resembling a giant's game board. Vance Warner's game board, Caryn reminded herself. The spikes of the perky pineapple plants embossed dark green against the red earth.

'Each plant provides three pineapple harvests,' Vance explained. 'The last is the

70

smallest but the sweetest.' He also reviewed some of the problems of pineapple agriculture and irrigation.

'Molokai played a joke on itself,' he commented at one point. 'The west end is flat and very dry, with sufficient water a constant problem, although some man-made reservoirs and pumping systems have helped. Water flows freely on the high hills of the north and east, with literally hundreds of waterfalls, but no way to capture it. And the east end is so densely jungled that the road barely penetrates its edge.'

'Yet the island's only thirty-eight miles long,' Caryn remarked, reciting her homework.

Vistas of ocean and beach and jumbled lava boulders constantly embellished their ride, and the emerald slopes of Maui beckoned across the stretch of sapphire water separating the two islands.

WindsEnd, Caryn discovered, spanned a good portion of the middle of Molokai. Its primary enterprise was cattle ranching, and Vance introduced her to a couple of the *paniolos*.

Around two o'clock they paused for lunch atop a hill distantly overlooking the main buildings of WindsEnd and the resort site. Caryn managed to scramble off her horse before Vance could again unsettle her with physical assistance. White ginger growing wild nearby permeated the air with a heady fragrance.

Vance spread their lunch on the blanket he'd unrolled: *lomi-lomi* (salmon with chopped onions and seasonings, he explained), papaya, pineapple spears, rolls, and coffee. The omnipresent breeze threatened to abscond with the plastic cups and plates until they were properly secured.

Vance slanted his head toward a couple of camper trucks, looking like toys, parked near the distant beach. Hardness tugged his lips. 'It looks like more of your workers have arrived.'

'Yes, we'll be getting into full swing next week.'

Caryn asked as they ate, 'You were born on WindsEnd? And have lived here all your life?'

'WindsEnd belonged to my father, and his father, and my great-grandfather, who was one of the last of the missionaries to come to Molokai in the late 1800s. I was born here, yes, but I didn't always live here.' Vance's gaze brooded across the ocean.

Caryn waited for him to continue if he chose, but didn't want to push.

Swiveling away, Vance plucked one of the white ginger blossoms. He rotated the flower's stem ever so tenderly between his middle finger and thumb.

Caryn speculated about feeling that hand, those fingers, on her skin—remembering the stimulation of Vance's earlier touches.

After a long pause Vance continued hesitantly, 'My mother left WindsEnd when I was three years old, and took me with her to San Francisco.' Clouds gathered in his eyes. 'Like you remarked your second night here, Molokai and WindsEnd can be boring for a woman. But I got to visit my father and WindsEnd every summer, and when I was thirteen, I announced that this was where I wanted to live. My mother finally agreed, though I think my father must have held the prospect of a court hearing over her head. By then I was old enough for the court to let me choose for myself.'

'Does your mother still live in San Francisco?'

'Yes, and she visits WindsEnd every year or two since my father died. But a week's about her limit for a stay here.' Again his eyes diverted from Caryn, studying the far green slope of Maui. 'She places fresh flowers on his grave every day she's here. I think she really loved him, but just couldn't adjust to this isolated living.'

'Sad, but I guess two people loving each other doesn't always make for a successful marriage.'

'Definitely not. But then marriage isn't everything, is it, Caryn?'

Both were half reclining on the blanket, leaning on opposite elbows and facing each other. Caryn was mesmerized as Vance

73

extended his arm and gently stroked his long fingers through her tawny hair before anchoring the white ginger blossom behind one ear. Caryn wondered if the side where he'd placed it signified she was 'taken' or 'available' in accordance with Polynesian custom.

Vance tilted her chin with his strong fingers and traced the outline of her lips, her cheeks, again her slightly parting mouth. He slowly, too slowly, moved his face toward hers till his handsome features filled her field of vision.

At last his lips touched hers, at first as softly as a butterfly's wings, then withdrawing, leaving her own lips almost trembling in their disappointment. Her free hand caressed upward along his tanned cheek and into his chestnut hair as he more firmly pressed his mouth to hers. Their kisses increased in length and intensity as Vance shifted his body closer to Caryn.

For moments they remained oblivious to the wind erupting more strongly around them and the gray clouds roistering about, multiplying across the horizon. Finally, a successful gust tipped coffee from a plastic cup onto Vance's arm.

Reluctantly detaching his mouth from Caryn's and glancing at the sky, he said, 'I guess we'd better start back.'

She stood near the edge of the hill for one last panoramic view as he loaded their picnic items back onto his horse. Then he came to stand behind her, his hands on her shoulders. She leaned against him, scarcely noticing her action because it seemed so natural, unaware of the wind blustering still more. His cheek nestled in her hair.

Languid in the pleasure of the moment, Caryn murmured, unthinking, 'It's all so beautiful. I don't see how you could bring yourself to sell any of it.'

She felt the immediate tautness in his body in the couple of seconds before he abruptly disconnected himself from her.

His voice moved away from her as he replied coolly, 'Let's just say your boss made me an offer I couldn't refuse.'

'I'm sorry,' Caryn started, but Vance proceeded away.

He watched to make sure she didn't have any trouble mounting, then galloped to the far end of the field before pausing for her to catch up. His palomino pranced about impatiently, as if expressing his master's mood.

They were on their way none too soon—in fact, not soon enough. Their pace had to be restrained because of Caryn's lack of horseback-riding experience. Yet the wind constantly collided face on with Caryn, slicking back her honey tresses and making it seem as if they were traveling at seventy miles per hour. Too bad horses aren't equipped with windshields, she thought.

A gust yanked the white blossom from her

hair, flinging it into the distance.

The rain began again, not the misty liquid sunshine for which Hawaii was fabled, but the torrents that tour books never mentioned but which Caryn had learned to expect of Molokai. Their environs became gray on gray, with visibility so poor that Caryn wouldn't have been able to find her way back without Vance in the lead.

When they finally rode into the stable, Vance asked with genuine concern, 'Are you okay?' He eased a wind-and-rain-battered Caryn off her horse, turning both horses over to a stable hand for care. Then he wrapped a dry blanket around the shivering Caryn. 'We'll wait a few minutes for the rain to let up before we make a run for the cottage.'

The downpour lessened five minutes later. As they sprinted in the direction of the cottage, the rain further subsided to a mild mist.

A few yards from the cottage Caryn slipped in the treacherous clay-colored mud, her sliding legs knocking Vance off balance too. In fact, his powerful body might have crushed hers beneath if he hadn't flung forward his arms in time to ease his plunge.

Their plight became hilariously funny to both of them. They both laughed for several seconds.

But desire bloomed and grew in their eyes. Gradually, their laughter abated, and a moment of silence heralded their passage into a higher realm.

Caryn's pulse gyrated faster than she thought possible, and her full breasts heaved with the deep breaths of passion.

Slowly, Vance lowered himself to her, molding her between his hard body and the resilient red earth. Caryn grasped him to her, vibrating, with his heartbeat echoing her own rhythm of life.

The surrounding platinum mist isolated them in an intimate dream world.

She wanted Vance. She needed Vance.

No amount of logic could displace the marvelous, unfamiliar sensations racing through every cell of her being.

'Caryn,' he murmured, and his probing tongue seared and twisted around hers. His powerful arms tunneled trenches in the soft mud beneath her shoulders, lifting her upward, pressing her to him still more.

Her breath tangled in her throat as he trailed kisses along its sensitive arch. Her hand meshed in his thick hair, impelling his face toward hers.

She kissed his cheek and nibbled at the lobe of his ear as he nuzzled the thrumming triangle at the V of her blouse and released the first buttons.

Beneath her the red earth seemed throbbing with life as they responded to a need more demanding and rapturous than they'd known existed, yet a need more primitive than the earth itself, more ancient than this volcanic island. A joining destined to span time and place.

As Vance seemed to have sprung from this land, so did they now both seem to become a part of it. Pressed between Vance and Molokai, Caryn pulsated between the two, melding into a part of both.

She tried to summon a protest. They couldn't continue. Not outdoors, in daytime, even though the platinum mist curtained them into a shimmering private world.

Abruptly, in a husky tone, Vance voiced Caryn's thoughts: 'We'd better go inside.'

A long moment wended past as nature was commanded to halt, while both struggled to regain some semblance of self-control and the strength to separate.

They couldn't let go of each other. Not yet.

What could I have been thinking? Caryn scolded herself.

She wasn't thinking. That was the trouble. She couldn't seem to think at all in Vance's vibrant presence.

Suddenly, Vance levered himself upward, his body severing from hers and exposing her to the chilling drizzle. Reaching down, he grasped her hands and extricated her.

Caryn was embarrassed by the obvious inverse sculpture of her figure in the mire, impressed there by Vance's body.

As the gray skies deluged her with reality,

Caryn reminded herself that the rain would delete her imprint in a matter of minutes, and Vance's mind probably would erase the memory of her with equal ease. She vowed that she too would rapidly erase both the physical and mental recollections.

That vow had hardly traveled through the corridors of Caryn's mind when they reached the cottage door, and Vance again gathered Caryn to him, his arms enfolding her tightly. Helpless, Caryn melted against him as his lips again sought hers.

Briefly detaching one hand from the slope of her hip, Vance opened the cottage door. As he started to guide her inside, Caryn frantically rummaged through her being for some shred of her earlier resolve.

'Vance, we can't.' But the words emerged on a sigh of desire.

'We can, we must,' he murmured amid kisses barraging all her senses.

I am Caryn Tallis. I am a cool, collected, tough construction superintendent—Caryn desperately recited the litany in her mind. I cannot become involved with a man—oh, such a man—but a man hazardous to my long-term emotional health.

'Vance, we have to stop,' she managed an urgent whisper.

'Why, Caryn, why?' His kisses and intensifying caresses continued their tender battering of her logic.

She grasped anxiously at the most obvious, simplest excuse. 'Not now. We're all yucky.'

Vance was not to be deterred by a little mud. 'I'd love to share a shower with you.'

Caryn took advantage of his slight pause to glide free of his kisses, then his embrace. 'I think I'd better shower alone,' she said, not at all certain she had the fortitude to enforce that decision if she received the slightest touch of protest from Vance.

But Vance merely looked at her as seconds filed past in a dirge to a lost opportunity, while his silver eyes attempted to plumb the depths of her soul.

'All right,' he agreed softly. 'Our first time should be perfect. I guess we'd better clean up.'

First time? No, there was to be no time for them—ever. Caryn knew she had to enforce that decision.

Or was he right? Was their joining inevitable? Written on the wind?

He backed away slowly, then pivoted and strode up the path toward his house.

Caryn stood beneath the shower for ages, as if its salvo could flood away the lingering sensations of Vance's touch. The red earth of Molokai clung to her like a stubborn reminder of her passion for Vance, until at last the final vestiges spiraled down the drain.

She could not so easily sponge from her mind the agitating concern about Vance's opinion of her—a wanton wench, willing to grovel in the mud for him.

At last she switched off the spray. As she reached to pull back the shower curtain, a rich male voice teased, 'It's about time. You must have dried up the reservoir.'

'Vance! What are you doing in here?!' Caryn was glad the shower curtain was of heavy, patterned plastic, not the see-through type.

But Vance seemed to see through her anyway. 'The front door was ajar. You didn't really mean to lock me out, did you, Caryn?'

Did she mean to lock him out, not only from her cottage, but from her life?

She should. But could she?

'I guess not,' she timidly mumbled an honest admission. 'But I'm not coming out of here until I've dried off and put on some clothes.'

'I'd love to perform the first function for you, but if you insist...' He pitched a towel over the shower rail.

Her subsequent request for clothing was answered by a sunny yellow sheet.

'Vance, I can't wear this.'

'Sure you can. That's my favorite outfit.'

He steadfastly refused all her pleas for normal clothing.

'I'll put this on if you'll get out of the bathroom so I have some styling space,' she eventually relented.

Vance kept his promise, Caryn confirmed as she poked her head tentatively around the edge of the shower curtain.

Once again Caryn tucked and folded and twisted the sheet into a sort of sarong/sari.

'Why don't you start a fire?' she called through the closed bathroom door.

'I thought we had.'

'It's chilly in here,' she insisted.

'Maybe it has become chilly,' he acknowledged with a cryptic sigh that reached beyond the confines of the wooden door.

Vance was seated in one of the chairs, facing the fledgling fire, when Caryn entered.

It looked so right: Vance sitting there, waiting for her.

'I knew I should have furnished this place with a sofa instead of two chairs,' Vance grumbled jestingly as Caryn slid into the other chair, which he'd pulled close to his own. 'I brought some wine, cheese, and fruit.'

Caryn smiled at his concession to other appetites. He too had vanquished the mud, and had changed into a russet silk shirt and pale fawn slacks.

Her eyes caressed the span of his broad, tapering back as he leaned forward to pour the wine into the crystal glasses he'd brought also.

'This is made from pineapples by a winery on the slopes of Haleakala, the dormant volcano that comprises much of Maui,' Vance explained. He also identified the assortment of exotic cheeses.

'You get all this on Molokai?'

'No way. The grocery stores only get *cottage*

82

cheese one day a week. When I fly to Honolulu a few times each month on business, I pick up special items.'

Caryn petulantly wondered whether Tami was among the special items Vance picked up whenever he traveled to Honolulu.

Such thoughts were exiled from her mind by Vance's fingers gently interlacing with hers.

They chatted for some time. Suddenly, every detail of the other's thoughts, tastes, feelings, and childhood and adulthood became urgently important. Tidbits of trivia to be stored in the recesses of the heart.

The room darkened while they talked for the next two hours, the only visible light issuing from the fireplace, though Caryn felt she must be glowing with Vance's presence.

Finally, he rose to add another chunk of wood to the fire. Instead of returning to his own chair, he moved behind Caryn's, and began tenderly rubbing her shoulders in a combination caress/massage.

Caryn watched the colorful, dancing flames in the fireplace lick at, race along, consume the logs. Just as flickers of desire licked at her, coursed through her being, set her ablaze.

Vance kissed the top of her head, and she arched her neck to raise her own half-parted lips in silent plea. He didn't deny her, obliging with a mouth that ravaged hers in the release of pent-up passion.

Eventually, his fingers slid down her one

bare shoulder, tenderly outlining the folded barricade of sheet.

'Caryn, Caryn,' he murmured.

She wanted him. She hadn't known it was possible to want anything or anybody as much as she longed to be fully joined to Vance Warner at this moment.

But what about all the moments hereafter? He offered her nothing permanent. She didn't want permanent attachments anyway—did she? She managed to move out of the chair, standing and facing him.

But her desire was written on her face, etched in the deepening blue of her eyes.

And he responded in kind, gathering her into his arms as he moaned her name again.

His mouth covered and possessed hers, as she willingly shared the honeyed recesses with him.

She felt as if she couldn't breathe. Yet breath was no longer necessary. Vance's had become her life's blood, with desire for him pounding through her every cell.

She pressed against him, glorying in the firm feel of his chest and grasping the powerful muscles of his back.

His powerful arms crushed her to him, molding the length of her compliant body to his. He kissed her long and deep, fully exploring her willing mouth. She answered his firmly demanding desire by adjusting her soft curve to him, educing a moan of aching need from his mouth mingled with hers.

Vance pulled away slightly, with a special smile that was for no one in the world but her. He murmured, 'You know, I'm almost glad you're here.'

Almost glad. The word 'almost' jammed in her mind, as if overloading and blowing all other circuits, trying to supplant all other sensations. Her brain frowned: *He was only kidding*. Of course. How foolish of her to get hung up on one word. Her body again relaxed and began to fully enjoy his caresses.

He tugged at the knotted sheet on her shoulder, attempting to free it. A tiny fragment of Caryn knew she should stop him.

But she couldn't, because his kisses were driving her into the wonderful oblivion of all-encompassing passion.

At last he succeeded in beginning to untie the knot holding the sheet in place. His whisper curled into the shell of her ear. 'At least we can enjoy each other for a few months.'

The soft yellow fabric began to slide, and she released Vance from her embrace just in time to halt its descent with a free hand, as her body stiffened noticeably beneath his touch.

For a few months. In the corners of her mind she must have recognized that was all it could be.

But it seemed so cold and calculated, like mechanical specifications on a blueprint, to point out, to *know* without doubt that their relationship was only to be for a few months. Vance was making it perfectly clear that she was nothing more than the most immediately available female.

Caryn's mind spiraled in a whirlpool of differing thoughts and emotions. Someday she'd have to deal with the realities of merging her own sensuality with career goals that didn't allow for marriage.

Why not today? Tonight. Here, with Vance.

But for such an affair to steam ahead without even a perfunctory discussion of love or a minor concession to the possibility of eventual marriage...

The winds of Molokai seemed to swirl her thoughts and emotions and physical sensations in a billion different directions. What do I want? What do I really want? Caryn asked herself.

Vance, Vance, Vance—the answer pounded back from every pore of her being. But someday—what about that someday, in a few months, when she would leave Molokai?

Vance's arms gently tried to dissuade her from moving away. But somehow she managed to step back, grasping the yellow sheet tightly and pulling it all the way up to her neck. She wanted to pull it over her head like a silken shroud, for pieces of Caryn Tallis seemed to die at that moment.

Disappointment and puzzlement battled with desire on Vance's features. 'What's wrong?'

'I, uh—I, uh.' Caryn swallowed hard. The raging sensations of her body, intensifying still with the so-near-and-yet-so-far presence of the source of her passion, were at odds with the logical judgment of her intellect. Her intellect triumphed at last. 'I've changed my mind.'

'Terrific. I always admire a woman who can make quick decisions.' His ragged breathing sounded a cacophony in her ear as he struggled for control, but he released his hands on her shoulders.

And suddenly she felt totally alone in a chill world.

Seconds trotted past before he said with cool evenness, 'Well?'

'Well what?' Caryn could scarcely think or speak at all, with all the emotional and physical feelings assailing her.

'I've never met a woman who was such a tease. I thought you wanted this as much as I did. Don't you think you owe me an explanation?'

'I don't have an explanation.' What could she tell Vance? She didn't fully understand herself.

A long moment slipped a wedge between them before Vance's next question issued forth, cold and bitter. 'I see you really do go for older men. Afraid you can't handle a virile young man?'

'What's that supposed to mean?' Caryn

defensively drew the sheet tightly around her, oblivious to its seductive outlining of her swells and curves. She couldn't bear to look at Vance, to let her eyes rove the magnificent terrain of his body.

'Just because I live in a remote location doesn't mean I'm naive or stupid. People your age don't usually have jobs at the level of responsibility of managing such a big project. Male or female. I know how you got this plum assignment. But I don't know how long you'll last in the job now that Jordan Nash's friendly persuasion is thousands of miles from Minneapolis.'

'You're despicable,' she sputtered at him, enraged with him and enraged with herself for sounding like a despoiled female in a Grade B movie. Then with a twinge of guilt for unfairly implicating her friend and employer, fifty-eight-year-old Jordan Nash, Caryn taunted, 'Maybe someday you'll learn that older men have a certain finesse, a certain *je ne sais quoi*.' She finished with a final thrust: 'I don't think I could even begin to explain it to you.'

Disbelief, anger, residual passion—all flashed through the silver eyes.

Displaying a composure she didn't feel, Caryn ambled to the bureau, acquired clean clothing, then sought refuge in the small bathroom, locking the door with a loud click. She turned on the shower to indicate that she intended to wash away Vance's touch.

Or to cover the sound of tears, as if the rise and flow of those tiny droplets could be heard in the next room.

I won't cry, Caryn determined. She hadn't cried since the death of her father. She refused to dispense one tear for such an arrogant chauvinist as Vance Warner. The salty dampness along her cheek must be spindrift from the nearby ocean.

Caryn threw the sheet on the floor and mechanically dressed in fresh jeans and a shirt without acknowledging that she should go to sleep soon anyway.

A long time passed before she heard the slam of the front door.

Caryn emerged, amazed to see Vance seated again in one of the chairs, though he had moved the two pieces of furniture far apart and faced them toward each other, as if for a council of war.

God help her. She wanted him still. Wanted him so much. Wanted to run across the room and throw herself at his feet, beg for his attentions and erotic ministrations. Beg for his love.

Instead, she managed to ask evenly, 'Why are you still here?'

'Because that's what I want to ask you—why?' Tortured dervishes whirled in the silver eyes to the tune of flickers from the nearby fireplace. 'I figured you wouldn't come out until you thought I'd left.'

'I have nothing to say to you.' She passively refused to sit in the opposite chair and face him. She lingered in the shadow of the corner.

'Why?' the question was wrung from the depths of his soul. 'I've watched you working. You're good at your job. Why would you sleep with Jordan Nash just to accelerate your career a little?'

Why with him and not with me? was Vance's real question, Caryn figured. Vance didn't love her. Only his ego rebelled at the thought of her with another man, and only then because he couldn't have her too.

'You're the one who insists on believing that's how I keep my job,' she pointed out with feigned matter-of-factness.

The tormented eyes sought her in the shadows. 'I heard some of Nash's men talking when they were here to close the sale. They very openly discussed Nash and his paramour in management on the company payroll.'

Caryn forced coolness through her tone. 'And did they tell you that her name is Sylvia Gianelli, and that she's the corporate vice president, and that she's had to endure phony rumors like that for years when there's no truth to them whatsoever?'

Am I now to be subjected constantly to those same toxic thorns of innuendo just because I'm a successful woman? Caryn wondered silently.

Vance bowed his head and roughly raked his hands through his thick chestnut hair. 'Caryn, what can I say?'

'"Sorry" is a nice though often ineffective word.'

She noticed he didn't exactly say it. Instead, he offered an excuse. 'I was upset—frustrated, to put it mildly. I just lashed out.'

'It wasn't entirely your fault. I should never have let things go so far between us. As you pointed out, I'll be here only a few months.'

Vance's body rose defeatedly from the chair like a giant sigh. 'Yes, you won't be staying on Molokai. It could be years before there's another commercial construction project here with a job for a top-flight superintendent.'

'It will be easier if we don't see much of each other.' Caryn voiced her feeling wondering if it was shared by him or if he could remain immune to her presence.

He acknowledged her wishes. 'We'll work something out so we don't run into each other at meals for a while. I don't want you living on snackables all the time.'

If I can live at all without seeing you. The thought pounced on Caryn's being.

He paused before her at the doorway. His fingers extended forth as if to trace her cheek, but retreated.

Leaving, Vance said softly, 'You're a construction superintendent skilled at building walls. Perhaps that's just as well. Molokai doesn't offer very stable ground for bridges.'

CHAPTER SIX

Tuesday morning the sun radiated across the sky without obstacle, and the breezes were calm, as if the spirits of the *kahunas* were appeased by Caryn's leaving Molokai, for even one day.

The propellors on Vance's Beechcraft were rotating as Caryn walked to Mike's smaller plane. Evidently, the Beechcraft was being warmed up by Vance's mechanic, because Vance himself appeared alongside the Cessna.

Today Vance looked more businesslike, but still devastatingly appealing, in a charcoal shirt and pearl gray suit, with the jacket flung carelessly over his arm. Caryn was glad finally to be expanding her own wardrobe, though most of her purchases would be of a strictly practical nature.

'You want to take off ahead of me?' Vance asked Mike. 'Ladies first?'

'"Bosses first" is my motto,' Mike replied jauntily.

Caryn considered protesting that Vance was neither hers nor Mike's boss, despite a demeanor that made him appear constantly in charge of everything, then thought better of making a big deal out of a casual remark.

'You go on. We're in no particular rush,' Mike continued.

They watched as Vance's plane moved down the runway, then rose like a huge, shiny bird against the horizon. 'Taxi, lady?' Mike quipped.

'Follow that plane, mister,' Caryn kidded as she climbed into the Cessna.

'You mean he's headed for Honolulu this morning too?' Mike asked, puzzlement in his tone as to why Caryn wasn't hitching with Vance if she knew his destination.

'I suppose so,' she dismissed.

Caryn noticed the Beechcraft when they landed, but Vance had disappeared. 'I guess about six would be the best time to meet you back here for the return trip to Molokai,' she said to Mike.

'No way, lady.'

'But I arranged the charter—'

'No way am I bringing you to Honolulu without treating you to dinner and a show or two.'

Sure, why not? Mike was pleasant company and Caryn would enjoy herself. 'Dinner will be great, but I can't make it too late a night, because I have to start working early tomorrow.'

'Okay, if that's the best I can do. Some Saturday night when I'm in your neighborhood, I'll drop down and pick you up and we'll see some shows.'

They agreed to meet at six-thirty at the top of the Ilikai Hotel. Caryn followed Mike's suggestion that she accomplish the bulk of her shopping downtown and at the Ala Moana Center, planning to do the tourist bit in the boutiques and gift stores lining Kalakaua Avenue in the Waikiki area later if she had sufficient time. She planned to take a few days off when the resort was completed to explore the attractions of Oahu before she left the Hawaiian islands forever.

She'd walked a short distance from the downtown Liberty House department store when a brief dose of Honolulu's 'liquid sunshine' shooed her under the arch of the closest doorway.

Minutes later when the misty rain became even lighter, Caryn hurried out of the doorway, nearly colliding with a passerby—a powerfully built passerby in a charcoal shirt.

Placing his hands on her shoulders as if to steady her, thereby making her feel totally unsteady, Vance kidded, 'I think I'm going to have to wear a suit of armor whenever it rains.'

Then I'll be sure to always carry a can opener, Caryn almost replied.

But before she could say anything, Vance's free-flowing jocularity suddenly froze, and his eyes stabbed silver icicles into her. 'We have a contract, Mzzzz. Tallis. And I intend to enforce it, with full legal action if necessary.'

He strode away before she could respond, leaving behind an astounded, confused, and timid little girl drowning in despair. In the next instant, though, the construction superintendent torpedoed to the surface. 'What the heck are you talking about now?' Caryn yelled to his departing back.

Vance pivoted, his long strides returning him in seconds. He gestured toward the building, glaring at her. 'Don't tell me you've hired all the qualified workers on Molokai yet!'

Turning, Caryn saw that the doorway in which she'd taken refuge belonged to an employment agency, with a sign in the window indicating construction and general labor among their specialties. Less than forty-eight hours after their last discussion, he was jumping to unwarranted conclusions about her again. At a loss for a lyrical expression of her feelings, she settled on a phrase she considered sufficient. 'Did anyone ever point out that you can be a real jerk sometimes?'

His anger boiled over. He now seemed the one unable to come up with a controlled statement while he paced the length of three steps back and forth in front of her. 'I'm a jerk?! I'm a jerk?!'

Caryn folded her arms before her and narrowed her eyes. 'Yes,' she confirmed.

His arm flung her direction in accusation. '*You're* the one flagrantly violating our written contract, which specified that former WindsEnd employees, then other Molokai residents, were to have hiring preference for the resort construction.'

95

'Oh, Vance, why don't you come in from the rain?' Caryn clued sarcastically.

His glare gradually faded with the dawn of comprehension, and he seemed to note for the first time her armload of packages. He said sheepishly, 'You just ducked into this doorway when the rain started?'

'Yes. I'll tell you that much, just once, because of the contract. Check it out for yourself, if you want to. I have shopping to do.' This time it was Caryn who pivoted and strode away.

Effortlessly, he caught up with her. 'Hey, it was an honest mistake.'

'You seem to make a lot of those.' She noticed 'sorry' had not yet invaded his vocabulary.

'Haven't you ever made a mistake, something that you regretted?'

'Yes.' She regretted becoming interested in Vance Warner, so that even his hint of a poor opinion of her was wrenching. But she didn't know how she could have staunched her interest at any point—certainly she'd tried.

Their pace had slowed to a normal stroll. Vance invited, 'Have dinner with me here in Honolulu tonight?'

'I can't. I have other plans,' she said politely, but without elaboration or discernible remorse.

'With Mike?' The question was asked hesitantly.

96

'It's really none of your business, Vance,' Caryn said without malice, though feeling slashingly cruel. 'We agreed last night not to spend a lot of time together.'

'That was your idea, not mine.'

'That's how it has to be, Vance.'

They paused at the intersection, Vance turning to reverse his route. 'Okay.' Then he imitated a hilarious Humphrey Bogart accent, 'See you around, kid.'

With a full load of packages Caryn arrived by cab at the Ilikai Hotel a few minutes before six, resolved not to think about Vance, not to wish she was with him instead of Mike tonight. She would have a wonderful time with Mike, whether she liked it or not, she determined with the same type of convoluted thinking that had inundated her since she'd met Vance Warner.

She stopped in the ladies' room to freshen up and change into the one splurgy and dressy purchase she'd made that day. If she'd known she'd be dining in style that night, she could have brought her splashy pink and orange island print with her from Molokai.

Although aware she'd never need two long dresses during her temporary assignment on Molokai, she wasn't sorry to have justification for buying this second frock. It too was an abstract island print, but in multiple shades of blue that complimented her eyes as well as contrasting nicely with her honey-blond hair. The V neckline pointed up certain of her other attributes, and the fabric was cool and soft and slithery.

Then Caryn embarked on the glass elevator, up thirty floors to what Mike had punned as 'Honolulu's top restaurant.'

Mike waited by the elevator. 'Wow,' he complimented. 'Lady, if I wasn't waiting for a rough, tough construction superintendent, I'd try to take you to dinner.'

'Well, fella,' she slipped her arm through his in mock seduction as she lowered her voice and eyelids appropriately, 'you think that tough construction worker would beat you up if you wined and dined me instead?'

'I'd wind up with bricks in my head either way.'

Mike disengaged his other arm from behind his back, where he'd concealed a gorgeous *lei* of lavender orchids interspersed with white plumeria. He fashioned the long, full flower necklace about her shoulders, then rested both hands there while he leaned forward and bestowed a kiss on each cheek. '*Aloha*, Caryn Tallis. Welcome to Honolulu.'

She gently fingered the delicate petals and breathed in the heady sweet scent of the plumeria. 'Thank you, Mike. I always wanted to experience this delightful custom. It's beautiful.'

They proceeded to their table in the glassy, classy restaurant. The views were awesome. Sunset glazed the horizon in deepest orange, and a line of *tiki* torches extending the length of Waikiki were already blazing the trail into nighthood. The once towering palm trees fringing the beach looked like toy props. A kaleidoscope of lights comprised the cityside scene. From here everything else seemed faraway and placid, perhaps because one was a wee bit closer to heaven.

Caryn found herself wondering where in that magnificent panorama was Vance tonight. Back on Molokai? With Tami, or with some other woman somewhere below? At least tonight she'd be above Vance Warner!

Caryn ordered a specialty drink to match both her attire and her mood, a Blue Hawaii. Then she determined to vanquish her melancholy and enjoy herself.

She sipped at her sweet-and-sour drink of orange curaçao, rum, and lime juice as she scanned the menu. After much vacillating between the gourmet choices, she decided on a Hawaiian *opakapaka*, a white fish fillet poached Marguery style with sauce Nantua, garnished with bay shrimp and mussels. Mike ordered the seafood brochette of prawns, snapper, salmon, and scallops.

As always, her time with Mike was very pleasant. Normally, she'd have more interest in such an attractive man. Darn Vance Warner!

'You seem farther away than those ants of people down below,' Mike interrupted her reverie.

'Sorry, I guess I'm just tired.'

'Tired of me?'

'No, of course not. Thank you for showing me a wonderful evening.' She felt a little guilty that he'd spent most of his charter fee on dinner.

'And you're not tired of Vance Warner either?'

'I don't know what you mean.'

Mike's interrogation was not combative, merely one of friendly concern. 'I mean I saw you two eyeing each other at the Mid-Nite Inn and again this morning. What's between you?'

'Nothing much.' Her statement was half true—the half that applied to Vance's viewpoint. To him she was merely a convenient transient.

'Then there's hope for me yet,' Mike ventured.

She wished there was, but didn't want to mislead him. She reached over and touched her fingertips to his. 'I'm sorry, Mike. I like you a lot, but I really don't want to get involved with anyone now. After all, I'll be leaving Hawaii in a few months.'

'So you're not interested in any relationship that isn't encircled with a wedding ring?'

'No, that's not it. Marriage really isn't for me. Apart from the constant relocating and other demands of my career, I'm not the domestic type.'

'You don't want short-term affairs, and you don't want long-term marriage.' Mike gently traced a finger along her cheek. 'Caryn Tallis, I think you're too warm a person to live forever without love, one way or the other.'

'That's not what I want.'

'Then what do you want?'

She felt uncharacteristically defeated, a strange symptom she'd experienced often in the last few days—and nights. 'I guess ... I don't know... I guess I want to want one or the other enough to be happy with that decision and lifestyle.'

'Poor Caryn.' Mike seemed genuinely sympathetic while trying to lighten her mood. 'Caught in a time warp between two eras ... I'm not exactly the settling-down type myself, but keep me in mind if your decision goes the other way.'

'Sure,' Caryn smiled back, 'you'll be right at the top of my list.' Not true, but it should be. At least Mike sincerely liked her, whereas Vance always wanted to believe the worse about her.

They capped their delicious dinner with frothy pineapple sherbet served in sparkling crystal, and Caryn found herself wondering if the fruit came from the red hills of Molokai.

She and Mike danced a couple of numbers, as far apart as brother and sister or two children at dancing class, before she said, 'We'd better be heading to the airport.'

'Let me call first. According to the earlier

weather reports, it was too windy around Molokai to be safe for small aircraft.'

When Mike returned from the telephone several minutes later, Caryn asked, 'What's the word?'

'"The answer, my friend, is blowin' in the wind." And the wind says no. But I was able to get reservations for the last show of the Polynesian Revue at the Beachcomber. We can check the airport again after that.'

Caryn was enchanted by the fast-paced and diversified show at the Beachcomber, featuring several Polynesian dances, including both the languid, graceful Hawaiian *hula* and the throbbing, more blatantly sensual Tahitian *hula*. The daring fire dancer with his twirling torches thoroughly enthralled her, but the flames seemed to leap across her mind to the blazing memory of another time, another place, another man.

At the Beachcomber they both drank specialty rum concoctions served in hollowed-out pineapples.

Mike checked with the airport immediately after the finale. 'Sorry,' he reported. 'We could catch the late show someplace else, then try again. But to be honest, the wind probably won't let up during the night, and I won't be too alert for flying by 2 A.M.' For emphasis he added, 'A Coast Guard helicopter crashed into a hill on Molokai one night a couple of months ago.'

Their next calls were no more successful, as they attempted to find a hotel room for Caryn.

One desk clerk explained, 'With the heavy snows burying the East and the Midwest for the past few weeks, a lot of Mainlanders are fleeing to any place where the only white stuff on the ground is sand.'

When it became obvious that only one place was available overnight, Mike jokingly placed his right hand over his heart, raised his left, and pledged, 'I promise I'll spend the whole night on the sofa.'

'Nonsense. I wouldn't want you to.'

Mike's features displayed a little disbelief as he tried to perceive her meaning. 'That was a quick decision.'

'Yes, I decided right away that *I'll* sleep on the sofa.' She smiled mischievously. 'I want you to be sure to get a good night's rest so you don't make a wrong turn tomorrow morning and land us in El Salvador or some such place.'

Briefly, Caryn wondered if Mike had passed on a phony weather report to lure her to his lair. She reminded herself that Mike had been extremely well comported toward her, and that she shouldn't let Vance Warner make her as suspicious of all men as he apparently was of all women.

The drive to Mike's apartment, located on the opposite side of the airport, took some time. His decor was contemporary renter. Unwashed dishes were in the tiny kitchen,

Caryn couldn't help noticing when she deposited her *lei* in the refrigerator. With pride though, Mike pointed out the tiny balcony of the living room from which, he claimed, the ocean, a quarter of a mile away, was visible in the daylight.

Caryn remained firm in her insistence that she would not put Mike out of his own bed. She stretched out on the sofa in the free-fitting, comfortable dress she'd been wearing.

Exhausted, she fell asleep immediately and remained semicomatose until she felt a strong male hand on her shoulder. Vance—he was with her again. She covered the hand with her own in a slow, sensuous caress.

Her shoulder oscillated. 'Caryn, keep that up, and I'll cancel my twelve o'clock customer. Come on, wake up, sleepyhead. We've got to get going.'

Stretching languidly, she forced her eyes half open. It was Mike, not Vance. It would never be Vance.

As if wielding smelling salts, Mike waved a cup of coffee under her nose. Instant—she'd recognize that distinctive lack of aroma anywhere. 'Up and at 'em. It's after nine-thirty. We haven't got much time if I'm going to get back to Honolulu by noon.'

She popped up. 'Omigosh, I should have started work before eight ... What about the wind?'

'I guess it either decided to let you back on

Molokai, or just plain got pooped out.'

Caryn didn't bother to change clothes for the return flight, figuring she'd get into a quick shower and a pair of clean jeans as soon as she arrived at WindsEnd. The slithery fabric didn't look slept in anyway.

As they drove to the airport, Mike mentioned, 'Hey, I forgot to tell you. The customers never showed for that sudden three-day charter that my answering service arranged the afternoon we were at the Mid-Nite Inn in Kaunakakai. After I waited in Honolulu a couple of hours, a messenger service arrived with a cancellation and a cashier's check for three days' fee anyway. So I made out on that deal.'

Mike completed the preflight check, and they were soon heading toward the land mass veiled by clouds in the distance, while the tiny-appearing city of Honolulu still could be viewed to the left in the bright sun. The Pacific was tranquil blue, merging from pale aqua to turquoise to deepest azure. From their height, the whitecaps scalloping the edge looked fixed and unmoving.

Soon the ruffled hills of Molokai came into focus, and they soared above ribbons of silvery waterfalls and streams sauntering through verdant valleys and into the sea. Then the Cessna pierced a hovering misty cloud and glided down to the WindsEnd airstrip.

Mike stopped just short of the hangar

occupied by Vance's Beechcraft, then came around to assist Caryn in disembarking from the plane.

'Do you need any help to carry all these packages to your cottage?'

'No, I can manage,' Caryn replied as she filled her arms with sacks and boxes. Thank goodness she'd mailed her aunt's birthday presents from Honolulu, even though it was much too early, instead of lugging them back here too.

'It was a great evening, Caryn'—Mike leaned over and gave her a brotherly peck on the cheek—'and you're welcome to spend the night at my apartment anytime.'

As Mike taxied the opposite direction for takeoff, Caryn juggled her packages, kneeing one maverick back into its proper but precarious position.

She was surprised to see Vance emerge from the twilight of the hangar. He must have been tinkering with his plane, Caryn decided, dismissing the hope that he might have been intentionally watching for her return. He couldn't have helped overhearing her and Mike.

Vance's features were a mask of impassiveness as he reached forward and fingered the smooth petal of an orchid, considerably less gently than she had, on the flower necklace she'd jauntily draped around her shoulders again that morning. 'Have a good time in Honolulu?'

The sarcastic tone of his query made Caryn consider dropping all her packages on his foot. But for a moment raw emotion showed on his features as he waited for her answer.

Nonetheless, she didn't stifle the response waiting on her lips. 'The best,' she said, smiling sweetly as she turned and strolled in the direction of her cottage with as much grace as she could fabricate while hauling an unwieldy load of packages.

Unfortunately, the packages exploded from her arms before she'd traveled far, scattering hither and thither on the ground. Vance rapidly closed the distance between them. 'I guess I can help you with these,' he grumbled.

'Don't bother. I don't need or want anything from you.'

He grasped her by the shoulders, guiding her sideways to face him. 'Well, I want something from you. And it's something you don't seem to mind making available to other men.'

His mouth came down on hers, not cruelly but with an intensity bespeaking desperate desire. Caryn steeled herself against any response, not entirely successfully. Vance drew back slightly to gauge her reaction.

She managed to sound cuttingly matter-of-fact: 'You have been watching old Bogart movies, haven't you? Or reading fifty-year-old romance novels. This island is decades behind in more ways than one. I guess you haven't heard that macho is out nowadays.' Even as she spoke, part of her longed for his lips to still hers, for his arms to bind her to him.

Vance looked both hurt and puzzled that his action hadn't produced the desired results. But his most agonizing dilemma was voiced by 'Why Mike and not me?'

Maybe it was best that he think she was involved with Mike. Maybe then they could avoid each other. Neither confessing nor denying, she said simply, 'I like Mike.'

'And you don't like me?' Vance prodded.

I could maybe love you, her thoughts admitted. That's the problem. Spending time with Mike doesn't endanger my career or my lifestyle, and doesn't expose me to possible pain.

She detoured around his question by pointing out coolly, 'You're the one who wants to believe I have something going with Mike.' She couldn't help adding a bitter taunt, 'Vance Warner—Champion Conclusion Jumper.'

'Caryn, I know you were gone all night, and I know what I saw and heard when Mike brought you home.'

His ashen eyes affected her like an injection of truth serum. 'It was too windy to fly back last night.'

'I managed to get back,' he started. Then, reluctant to fire the first shot in a new battle, conceded, 'But that was midafternoon.'

'I slept on Mike's couch because the hotels

were all full.' Drat those independent vocal cords of hers. Why couldn't she have kept her mouth shut and maintained whatever sanctuary was offered by an imagined affair with Mike.

Vance's silver eyes flowed into hers. His lips pressed together and inverted in an unsuccessful attempt to lock in his forthcoming statement. 'Caryn, about this morning—and yesterday afternoon, and Sunday night—I'm'—the last word bumped through his lips with difficulty, as if seldom having occasion for such an excursion—'sorry.'

'Thank you,' Caryn responded simply, both touched and surprised.

'Want to demacho me now?'

'You make that sound really obscene,' she bantered back, delighted that their inherent, humorous rapport had resurfaced.

'Well, if you refuse to give lessons, just tell me if I'm getting it right.'

Slowly, tentatively, Vance gathered Caryn into his arms, and she was neither able nor willing to contest his action. Once again he lowered his lips to hers, applying slight, exquisite pressure and movements. His tongue lazily tantalized her lips to open.

Caryn's brain struggled ineffectually to transmit orders to the rest of her body. When she placed her palms against Vance's chest to push him away, they were unable to move as they absorbed the marvelous feel of him, the rise and firmness of his muscles, the warmth of his skin, the rapid throbbing of his heart...

His tongue glided along her lips, begging admission...

A merging that could only escalate a need for an even deeper merging.

Somehow Caryn dredged up the fortitude to pull back. He didn't try to restrain her.

'I think you've got it,' she tried to say lightly.

'But you don't want it.'

'Vance—'

'I know. We've got to stop meeting like this,' he semikidded.

'Right.'

'Right.' He added pragmatically, 'You're already late for work. You have unfinished walls waiting for you.'

CHAPTER SEVEN

The first structures erected were the company-owned modular buildings that had been shipped in for the field office and temporary housing for the employees who found it more convenient to reside at the site. About half the workers made the long commute from the opposite end of the island each day, and most of the others returned to their homes on the weekends.

110

During the next few weeks the construction progressed rapidly.

Sometimes when she glanced up from her clipboard, Caryn's heart stumbled over the sight of a tall, powerful figure of a man standing just inside his own property line. Or sitting astride his horse, silhouetted against the horizon, on the far hill—their hill, she had come to think of it.

But by mutual accord they avoided contact. Caryn usually breakfasted on toast and coffee at her cottage, was furnished by Hira with bounteous sack lunches, and worked late enough to avoid dinner except for a snack in the cottage or a microwave-heated plate of leftovers from Hira.

A tiny refrigerator and microwave oven had magically appeared in her cottage. Was Vance concerned about her nutrition? Or did he really not want her around?

She ate at the main house only when she knew Vance was away from WindsEnd. As he had been with increasing frequency, often flying to and remaining in Honolulu.

Employee hiring had been completed, and the work zipped along with full crews. But many of the workers were sullen toward Caryn, Kano being among the few exceptions. Caryn was uncertain how much they resented her for being an outsider and how much for being a woman. She tried to elude the paranoic feeling that John Umeshi was intentionally spreading discontent among the workers. She had no actual proof, but his sexist attitudes were blatantly apparent when they were alone.

John, as well as many of the other men, had been particularly unhappy when she'd hired three females for some general labor and eventual painting. Two of them were married to older Filipino immigrants and the third was a semireformed *haole* hippie—but they all fulfilled the requirement of having lived on Molokai for some time. Caryn had to be especially careful not to show them any preference and thus was unable to initiate even casual friendships. The two Filipinos spoke little English anyway, and Caryn hadn't much in common with a self-proclaimed hippie.

The care she had to exercise in her dealings with the three women employees annoyed her, because no one would make anything of a male boss acting as mentor to a select few other men.

At least a small percentage of the male workers now accorded her a grudging respect, having witnessed her expertise, and no one was about to ignore her orders with the current employment situation. Caryn suspected Kano was trying to help eradicate the discontent sown by John. But since John was Kano's direct supervisor, there wasn't much Kano could do overtly.

Caryn also suspected John coveted her position. He didn't realize that Resorts Inc. would simply send someone else from their headquarters if she left this project for any reason.

Caryn would have enjoyed an occasional early morning or evening swim in the ocean. But that was out of the question. Permitting labor to ogle management might lead to problems.

Instead, she drove on Sundays to other beaches on Molokai. And occasionally the construction came to a total halt for twenty minutes or so if a group of whales migrated through the channel between Maui and Molokai during working hours. Otherwise Caryn had little recreation except for an evening stroll along Resorts Inc.'s beach or curling up with a novel, but she didn't have much time for fun and games anyway.

Exhausted from the day's work, she was returning to her cottage one evening when she heard the sound of a small aircraft. She wondered if Vance was taking off.

If so, perhaps she could have a nice dinner in the kitchen at the main house with Hira, who now seemed much happier, though only a tad more communicative. But she also considered that Hira might want to have dinner alone with Kano.

Caryn was debating whether to bother Hira when she heard a cheerful 'Hi' from halfway down the path. She turned to see Tami waving at her in greeting.

'You are joining us for dinner tonight, I

hope?' Tami invited.

Oh no. But Caryn wanted Vance to think she could be indifferent, not intimidated by his presence nor upset at seeing him and Tami together. Tonight could be a prime demonstration if she could pull off the act.

'I'll look forward to it,' Caryn smiled back. 'Please ask Hira to set a place for me.'

Selecting a short-sleeved chemise of buttercup piqué from her closet, she tried to convince herself that she had no intention of reminding Vance of his 'favorite outfit' in a different shade of yellow. Caryn was surprised to note six settings on the table when she entered the cherry-wood dining room.

Vance was mixing cocktails at a small bar which had been discreetly concealed behind the paneling on the other occasions Caryn had dined in this room. Vance looked very appealing in his usual blue jeans and a short-sleeved tropical print shirt.

John and Kano were the other guests, also informally attired. John was physically well built, indeed quite handsome. But he so obviously considered himself a reward to the world in general and women in particular that Caryn couldn't imagine anybody electing to spend one unnecessary moment in his company. However, as long as he competently performed the duties of his job, she had no justification for terminating him, and refused to let personality conflicts dictate her business

114

decisions.

Tami wore a short sundress of flowered green fabric, with her lustrous black hair trailing halfway down the smooth amber skin of her exposed back. Hira was even joining them all for dinner, wearing a lovely tropical print dress.

Caryn couldn't squelch the urge to order pineapple wine as her drink when Vance inquired. Their fingers brushed as he handed her the glass, and remained lightly touching for several heartbeats. She wondered if he too was remembering the last occasion he'd served her this wine.

He was. Vance attempted to break the spell with humor, and assistance from Humphrey Bogart. A twitching corner of his mouth heralded the imitation: 'Of all the gin joints in all the towns in all the world, she had to walk into mine.'

Caryn laughed, but her emotions questioned: Ingrid, how did you ever manage to get on that plane?

A marvelous array of food was set out buffet style on a sideboard in the dining room, and a built-in warming tray held multiethnic cuisine, including sweet-and-sour pork, *mahi-mahi*, beef *sukiyaki*, and fried rice. Fresh sliced papaya, pineapple, and mangoes were available, along with tossed salad incorporating several vegetables. Everything tasted exquisite—especially to hot-plate

115

Caryn.

The conversation was general. Vance and Caryn calculatingly ignored each other as much as possible, and the others tried to ignore that.

Only John failed to comply with the overall tone of the evening. He absolutely leered at Tami much of the time, the obviousness of his passes and the off-color hue of his remarks increasing in direct proportion to the number of bourbons he consumed.

Tami handled him extremely well, and Caryn had no doubt that such tact in dealing with obnoxious lechers was Part I of any flight-attendant course. Nonetheless, John was making the evening unpleasant for everyone, and Vance looked ready to punch him out.

'John,' Caryn insisted at an opportune point, 'I just thought of something I need to know about the work that was completed today. I don't want to bore everyone at the table with shop talk. Why don't you step over to the bar with me for a minute, and pour us both another drink?'

Petulant, John followed Caryn to the far corner of the room.

As he reached for the bourbon bottle, Caryn murmured so the others couldn't overhear, 'Back off, John.'

John didn't react immediately, merely splashing liquor into his glass. Then he mumbled, not looking at Caryn, 'I don't know

116

what you mean.'

'I mean leave Tami alone. She's made it clear that she's not interested in you, and your constant come-ons are making everyone else uncomfortable too.'

John glared at Caryn with undisguised loathing. 'We're not on the job now, boss.'

'On or off the job, you represent Resorts Inc. Apart from their influence on the other islanders, these people are our neighbors. In fact, Resorts Inc. is still negotiating with Vance Warner to purchase additional property for a full eighteen-hole golf course. Your actions are hardly fostering good relations.'

John crooked up one corner of his mouth in a half leer. 'That's exactly what I'm tryin' to do, boss—foster good relations.'

Caryn said levelly, eye-to-eye since John wasn't much taller than her own five feet eight inches, 'You heard me, John. From now on you treat Tami as if she were your grandmother, except don't even ask her to so much as bake a batch of cookies.'

John's eyes became narrow, dark slits. 'Is that a firm order, boss?'

'You want it in writing?'

Though the hard muscles in his body remained tensed, his words became cooperative. 'Now I understand you, boss. You got it. No more Tami for me.'

When the party broke up later, Tami caught Caryn's hand momentarily and whispered,

'Thanks for whatever you said to John.'

Caryn squeezed her hand in return and smiled, murmuring, 'Thank you for not throwing us all out of here.'

John had been the first to leave.

Caryn picked her way along the path to her cottage, pausing to breathe in intermingling fragrances of thousands of blossoms.

With the full moon sufficiently lighting her way, Caryn didn't bother to switch on the flashlight she'd learned to always carry in her oversized purse. She didn't notice John leaning against the front of the cottage until she was nearly at the door. 'What are you doing here?'

'No more games, boss. I'm right where you want me to be. Your orders, remember?'

'I don't know what you're talking about,' it was Caryn's turn to say. She faced John directly, automatically steeling herself and tightening her fingers on the key she'd held ready to unlock the door.

Much of John's muscular body was sheathed in shadows, and his facial features weren't discernible. 'You've been playing the ice maiden for weeks, but tonight you made it clear you want me for yourself, and I'm tired of waiting.'

John lunged at her, clamping her body in his arms and trying to cover her mouth with his in a sloppy, wet, and rough kiss. His false assumption that she wanted this and his locked-in stance with legs slightly apart enabled Caryn's action.

She brought up her knee, hard, and simultaneously raked her key across John's cheek. She followed through by pivoting her body at an angle to his as he yelped and leapt back like a dangerously wounded animal, left paw gingerly feeling the scratch along his cheek and right paw covering his other injured spot.

'Now you're really gonna get it,' he growled.

'Eager to spend some time in a jail cell, John?' Caryn maintained an appearance of calmness, with a cool tone in her voice contrary to the anger and fear rising inside her.

'Who'd believe you?' his growl continued, low and primitive and threatening. 'You're no Snow White. I saw you myself, groveling right here in the mud for Vance Warner, ready to let him take you right here where all the world could see.'

So their shimmering platinum curtain had been transparent after all.

'And again that day on the airstrip. You were ready to have that pilot and Warner both in a row.'

His statements nauseated her, but she jabbed back, 'But you're neither Vance Warner nor Mike O'Riley. You're just superobnoxious! And I can't stand the sight of you.'

'Everybody knows your type, and people saw you demand me for yourself tonight. Nobody will believe you didn't want this.'

He lunged at her again, but with her body sideways to his, she didn't present a broad and easy target. Extending her arm with as much force as possible, she hit the small bone between his nostrils with the heel of her hand. With a cry of pain, John staggered backward a couple of steps, then folded to his knees. Had refuge not been five feet away, Caryn would have followed through with a few more moves she knew.

For what seemed hours she fumbled to place her key in the cottage door, thinking she heard other noises. Did John have an accomplice, approaching from a different angle?

Actually, only a few seconds passed before she attained the sanctuary refuge of the cottage, immediately relocking the door behind her. She leaned against its sturdy panel, trembling uncontrollably in a combination of fear and rage as she listened for sounds outside, for any clue that John was going to attempt to break in.

She considered screaming, but thought she was too far from both the main house and the workers' housing for anyone to hear her. Besides, she was no longer in immediate danger.

No disturbance nor sound of any kind initiated from outside during the ensuing hour. Caryn remained seated numbly in a chair in front of the weeks-cold fireplace with her hand wrapped around the poker.

She wanted so badly to go to Vance. To seek his comfort and protection. But she knew she couldn't do so even without the possibility that John might still be lurking outside.

She had to constantly remind herself that, though he had more finesse and the good grace not to force himself on her, Vance was no different from John in one way—Vance too wanted Caryn just temporarily without deep caring.

She hardly slept at all that night, afraid to let down her guard, and kept the poker in bed alongside her—a poor substitute for a knight in shining armor.

The next morning in the small aluminum prefab building serving as the field office, Caryn was reviewing the week's schedule with Kano when John arrived late.

'What happened to your face?' Kano asked on seeing the angry red scratch extending the length of John's cheek.

'I'd say he must have run into some thorny problem while fumbling around in the dark last night,' Caryn icily preempted John's reply.

And when John turned the other cheek in her direction, Caryn was amazed to see a large bruise she didn't remember bestowing.

'Kano, go check on them women workers,' John ordered. 'You got to keep an eye on them all the time.'

Kano looked to Caryn with uncertainty.

'Go on and keep to the schedule I gave you,'

Caryn half countermanded.

Caryn glared at John with unmitigated hatred, which he reciprocated. As soon as Kano was out the door, Caryn started, 'If you ever again—'

'You can't fire me,' John interrupted. 'I already told half the guys that you begged me to bed you last night and got really mad when I refused.'

Caryn was agape with shock.

'I'm a married man, you know.'

'I didn't know,' Caryn's tone was thick with anger and sarcasm, 'but the only thing surprising about that bit of news is that any woman would have you.'

She continued in a frosty, businesslike tone, 'It was not my intention to fire you this morning. We're not in the military service where you're automatically discharged for laying a hand on a superior,' she emphasized the last word. 'I have taken into consideration the fact that last night's incident did not occur during business hours, that you were drunk, and that a full moon no doubt affects the behavior of types like you. However, you are now officially on probationary employment status. If you so much as accidentally brush against me or even make a snide remark, you're fired. If you harass any other woman on this entire island, either verbally or physically, you're fired—but then that should be no problem for you since you're so intent on being

122

faithful to your dear wife. And your job performance better be *perfect*—I don't need much incentive to get rid of you.'

She reached down and straightened a sheaf of papers on the desk, feigning total indifference to his recent bombshell. 'As for the ridiculous story you claim to have told the men this morning, I imagine they're all having a good laugh at you right now. Everyone knows you chase anything in skirts, just as they know I would have no interest in a man of your caliber. Now get out of here and get to work.'

John's dark gaze was vitriolic, but he complied with her order without comment.

As soon as he left, Caryn slumped down in the chair behind the desk, a pencil trembling between her fingers. She didn't believe a word of her last statements to John.

She feared the men were all laughing and whispering about her now.

Caryn had decided not to have John arrested for attempted assault because it would be bad for the image Resorts Inc. was trying to create on Molokai.

She hadn't fired him for reasons involving her own career image, not because of any question of his word against hers. She simply didn't want Jordan Nash and the other corporate executives to think that a woman couldn't handle this job, that a woman couldn't properly supervise and control male employees, that a woman's presence on a job site caused special problems. She certainly wasn't going to permit John Umeshi to affect her career prospects, and those of other women.

In fact, she was sending no written report of his 'official' probation to headquarters. It would remain in a private file in her cottage in case she ever needed it.

The men, though more desultory than usual, followed Caryn's instructions over the next few days. John fulfilled his duties and kept his distance.

The exterior and partial interior were completed on the building at the west of the trio of lodgings; and the exterior of the center building was nearing completion. They were referred to, unimaginatively, as Building No. 1 and Building No. 2.

The other employees had ended their workday two hours earlier when Caryn took a perfunctory glance at the materials waiting in readiness for the interiors. Astonished at what she found, she rushed back to the field office and checked the receipts.

She began the next morning by questioning the employee whom she instinctively trusted most, Kano.

Later she summoned John Umeshi into her office. He started to sulk into the chair across from her desk when she interrupted icily, 'Don't bother to sit down. You aren't going to be here that long.'

Defiantly, John plopped down anyway.

'Your theft has been discovered. I've consulted with Jordan Nash in Minneapolis by phone, and he has informed me that they don't want to blemish the Resorts Inc. image by insisting on a criminal investigation and prosecution. If it were up to me personally, I'd campaign for as long a jail sentence as the laws permit. Your action could have cost lives someday.'

While John constantly denied everything and challenged her to 'prove it,' Caryn outlined what she'd discovered and traced. John had been substituting inferior materials, no doubt selling the better materials at a profit to some shady contractor who didn't care where he got them.

After detailing other substitutions, she stood, slapping a stack of papers against the desk in anger. 'And your substitution of smaller No. 16 copper wire for No. 12 copper wire could have started an electrical fire someday—a fire that might have killed people because of your petty greed! I can't understand the perverted thinking that would consider a few thousand dollars worth human lives!'

John continued his sneering denials until it became obvious that Caryn had indeed accumulated sufficient proof against him.

'In case you hadn't guessed by now, you're fired. Get your stuff together and be off this site by noon. If you ever again step one inch inside

Resorts Inc.'s property line, I'll have you arrested.'

As he sidled to the door, John's features twisted and he growled through yellowed teeth, like a cornered animal. 'I've already been tellin' the men how you've continued to harass me, hot for my body. I'm gonna make sure they know I was fired by a frustrated female.'

Caryn was so furious that she tried three times to vent her anger by snapping a pencil in half before she noticed it was a ballpoint pen.

* * *

The employees didn't seem to treat her any differently. A few even seemed to accord her more respect.

Yet she couldn't help wondering what they were thinking. Were any of them whispering behind her back about John's allegations?

Caryn constantly told herself, 'Chin up,' and 'Take it on the chin,' and 'Keep a stiff upper lip,' and other facial clichés that didn't even make sense, much less help. Somehow she managed not only to keep going, but to maintain a thoroughly professional demeanor. For the next few days she took over John's duties as well as her own, involving more direct supervision of the workers.

Despite the restiveness, within those days the project got back on schedule, even recouping some of the time lost earlier due to

126

inclement weather. Caryn tumbled into bed after each sixteen-hour workday too fatigued to ruminate about her personal problems.

At the end of the week she promoted Kano to John's position as assistant superintendent, and told him to select a new general foreman, whoever he felt best qualified among the other workers. Kano chose a bantamweight but competent man of Filipino descent named Esidoro.

When she made the promotion announcements to the assembled workers just before quitting time on Friday, they seemed pleased.

Caryn had spent most of Saturday updating the cost records when Kano came into the office.

'You're supposed to be off today,' Caryn tiredly smiled a greeting. 'Only us big bosses work on weekends.'

Kano plunked a paper bag down on her desk. 'Your lunch,' he decreed. 'I had Hira make you a sandwich. You've hardly been taking time to eat lately, and this will hold you until the *luau* tonight.'

'What *luau?*'

'My friends, the Manukeles, are having a *luau* in honor of their twenty-fifth anniversary. A lot of the islanders will be there, including some of our employees.'

Caryn's expression fell. 'I can't go, Kano.'

'Why not?'

'Well, for one thing, I wasn't invited.'

'I just invited you. Island *luaus* are very open. Everybody's welcome.'

Not me, Caryn thought. 'I have some work I have to do tonight,' Caryn fumblingly semilied.

'Come with me, and I'll help you with it tomorrow. An old Hawaiian fossil like me doesn't often get a chance to escort a beautiful young woman.'

'You're sweet to ask, Kano, but I can't.'

Then Kano cut the small talk. He reached both bronze arms across the desk and took Caryn's hand between his own in grandfatherly fashion. 'I know why you don't want to go, Caryn. But you must try to ignore John's lies. I've done what I can to refute them, and only a few believed him anyway. As for tonight, it takes a lot more class to show up than to hide away.'

That night she wore the splashy, flashy pink and orange abstract print bought in Kaunakakai weeks before.

On the job she only wore lipstick and sunscreen lotion. But tonight she applied full makeup, including an ivory foundation and artistically applied blushers in two different shades. Never in favor of heavy-looking eye makeup, she smoothed on light 'eye-opener' eye shadow after blazing an ultrathin trail along the outer edges of her lashes with dark eyeliner. She filled in and slightly accented her eyebrows with a brush-on, then finished with black mascara.

Blow-dried and brush-styled into a bouncy flip, her tawny hair shone, reflecting honey highlights.

For her jewelry she selected the polished pearl on a delicate gold chain that Ben had sent her from the Orient last Christmas.

The overall effect was festive and—she'd even say so herself—rather attractive. Too bad her mood didn't match.

They drove almost an hour in Kano's jeep before turning onto a narrow dirt road that eventually wound its way to the *luau*.

Over a hundred people milled about the landscaped grounds of a modest home. Kano introduced her to the hosts, his friends who'd been married for twenty-five years—no doubt an anomaly on Molokai from the tales she'd heard of divorces.

She felt badly about not bringing the Manukeles a gift, but there was no place to shop between WindsEnd and here. She determined to buy something in Kaunakakai or Honolulu at the next opportunity, and have Kano pass it along to this couple, who proved very charming and hospitable.

She recognized many of the guests. Most of the employees felt obligated to introduce their wives and children, but it was obvious that she wasn't truly welcome by anyone except the hosts and Kano, and was throwing the proverbial wet blanket on the entire celebration. The islanders hadn't exactly given Caryn and her project their wholehearted approval and support even before John's lies.

Kano remained stalwartly at her side until he noticed Hira depositing a dish of food on the enormous buffet table. 'Go ahead and talk to her,' Caryn insisted, adding the fib, 'I'll be fine.'

Kano hesitated but capitulated. 'Okay. I'll be back in a few minutes.'

Conventional electricity floodlighted the buffet table, but *tiki* torches provided dramatic illumination for the rest of the large yard. Caryn decided to move toward the front where it wasn't as crowded.

Then she saw him, chatting with the hosts. Vance wore white chinos with a short-sleeved chocolate-colored shirt unbuttoned halfway down, in keeping with the casual *luau* atmosphere. The flickerings of flaming *tiki* torches licked across the exposed portion of his chest and burnished the reddish-brown hairs just as the blaze in her cottage fireplace had done on that night so many weeks ago.

He looked delicious. Manly and totally appealing. Irresistible. That was the right word. Irresistible. Caryn knew in that instant that she wouldn't be capable of denying Vance Warner nor herself if he ever again tried to make love to her.

But he wouldn't. Instinctively, Caryn looked

around for Tami, who wasn't with Vance at that moment. Caryn was sure she'd appear soon, looking stunning as always.

Now Caryn felt doubly dismayed. She hadn't expected Vance to be here tonight.

Retracing her steps, she picked her way the opposite direction around the far end of the house, making herself inconspicuous in the shadows beneath a majestic tree aburst with bright red blossoms.

She was leaning unhappily against its trunk when a man murmured beside her, his breath warm in her ear, 'You rival that flame tree in brilliance and beauty.'

She prepared to confront a new antagonist, some man who'd believed John's lies and pinpointed her as a sure target for tonight. But there was something reminiscently tantalizing about the timbre of that voice...

'Vance'—she couldn't restrain the excitement in her own voice—'uh, hello,' she finished feebly. He wasn't even touching her, but she felt as weak in the knees as a ninety-year-old who'd just run the three-minute mile. Nervously, she glided a pink tongue over her lower lip, only belatedly aware of the suggestiveness of that gesture.

'Don't you mean *aloha?*' His silver eyes gilded her. '*Aloha* is such an all-encompassing word. It can mean hello, or love—'

'Or goodbye,' she added softly but pointedly.

'I see you're learning our Hawaiian culture. Then perhaps you've realized that you're a *wahine* and I'm a *kane*, and together we can be—' He pressed his lips to hers, and she reveled in that small contact of skin on skin, in the scent and the taste of him, still familiar after all these weeks.

That gentle yet intense kiss seemed to last forever—until an alarming thought awakened her dormant mentality.

'Are you here because of John Umeshi?' she asked breathlessly, fearfully. Perhaps Vance was just another of the men who considered her easy pickings—in fact, he'd thought that even before John made sure everyone on Molokai heard his false tales.

'That...' Vance uttered a series of angry expletives. 'I'd have been by your side a week ago if I'd known what filthy lies he was spreading. I just found out about it today, when Kano came to assure me it wasn't true. I'm putting a stop to any phony gossip, not that I expect too many people bought his story anyway.'

'Then you do believe in me,' she said, half to herself, thrilled to hear it. After she'd behaved so wantonly with Vance in the past, she'd worried he might presume she'd be the same way with John. Or was it just an ego thing, Vance's knowing that she would hardly turn him down, then pursue John.

'Why do you believe in me?' she prodded

132

quietly, eager to hear that he thought well of her, that he trusted her—yes, that he loved her. She wanted and needed to hear that he loved her, because she'd been afraid for some time that what she felt for Vance was love.

'Because I saw how you treated John that night after dinner in front of your cottage.' At her look of astonishment Vance explained, 'I was coming to thank you for whatever you said to make him stop pestering Tami.' As her expression became even more aghast, he admitted sheepishly, 'Well, it was an excuse to see you alone.'

Not perceiving the depth or cause of her incredulity, Vance continued: 'I was shocked when I saw from the distance the two of you, John's arms around you. I was torn between coming closer to overhear your conversation, or withdrawing to leave you alone as I thought you wanted. But in the next few seconds you made it clear you didn't want to spend any time with him.'

'Well, thanks so much for all your help that night,' she said caustically. That explained the noises of distant approach she'd heard.

'You always claimed you didn't want nor need any help from me, Caryn. And you didn't seem to require any that night. You had the situation resolved before I could have even reached you.'

'Haven't you ever heard of emotional support?' her words sounded tremulous.

'I didn't know you wanted or would accept that from me either. In fact, I figured you wouldn't even let me in the door after just fighting off one lecher.'

Her mood eagerly assuaged by his excuses, she asked hesitantly, kiddingly, 'Is that what you are—another lecher?'

He interlaced the fingers of his large hand with her smaller one, and smiled. 'I guess I am where you're concerned.'

She couldn't say which of them made the next move. Suddenly, she was melting into him, malleable within the tight circle of his arms.

'What kind of tree did you say this is?' her lips were a whisper away from his.

He glanced up as if he'd forgotten, puzzled at her question. 'A poinciana.'

'No, before you called it a flame tree. Something's setting me on fire, and I just wondered what to blame,' she teased.

'Blame me, darling. Or should I say "Credit me"? Only me, I hope.'

Their mouths merged totally, exploring and delighting in each other, and both were desperate for that same merger of their total beings. Caryn felt as if she were cast of gelatin.

A fanfare of Tahitian drums from the backyard so echoed the throbbing Caryn felt that she thought she might have imagined it.

'They're getting ready to take the pig out of the *imu*,' Vance explained, moving to her side

134

and keeping his arm about her waist as he guided her toward the backyard. She felt much too giddy to think about food.

Vance added a point of clarification that made her even giddier. 'I suppose I ought to tell you that I got to Umeshi after you were safe inside the cottage. Suffice it to say I made it clear that he'd better not so much as sneeze in your presence in the future.'

The source of John's bruise was identified— one effective punch, no doubt. So instead of a physical offensive, John had mounted a verbal assault from behind her back. But John Umeshi was, as far as Caryn knew, far away from WindsEnd and back with his long-suffering wife.

Vance continued haltingly, gazing into the distance rather than looking directly at her. 'Then I waited up half that night for you to come to me—for emotional support or physical protection or anything. But you never came. I had to face the fact that you really don't need me.'

Caryn didn't know what to say but, with her hand, covered and pressed his hand that was resting at her waist.

Since the area was already crowded for the traditional *luau* ceremony, Vance assisted Caryn up onto a chair where she could watch from the far edge of the yard. Four men poured water over smoking hot rocks as Vance commentated, 'The pit is called an *imu*. The carcasses of pigs are stuffed with heated rocks; and the pigs, along with wire baskets filled with sweet potatoes, are surrounded and covered over with more hot rocks; then the pit is sealed under layers of wet banana and ti leaves, burlap, and earth. After it bakes an entire day, the pork is so succulently tender that it hardly stays on the fork long enough to reach your mouth.'

Vance helped her down from the chair, and they filtered to the edge of the line forming for the buffet table, their fingers entwined.

'Hi, gee, I didn't mean to get here so late, but I had a last-minute charter.'

Vance dropped Caryn's hand as they both saw Mike. 'I didn't know you'd be here,' Vance feigned casualness.

'I had a special invitation,' Mike grinned at them.

Caryn had no idea what Mike was talking about. She hadn't known about the *luau* herself until this afternoon.

'If you'll excuse me, now that you're here to guide Caryn through the feast, I see some friends I really should talk to.' Vance left Caryn agape and miserable.

Vance never learned. He hadn't even afforded her the opportunity to clarify the situation. Since he wasn't interested in her explanations, she certainly wouldn't force any on him. This was for the best anyway, she comforted herself, disbelieving her own

136

platitude.

'Mike, would you take me home now?' Caryn asked.

'What? We haven't eaten yet!'

He was right. Like Kano had said earlier, showing up was classier than hiding away. Well, she'd show up Vance Warner by enjoying Mike's company along with a good meal.

The long table burgeoned with dishes brought by many of the guests. Alongside the pork sat chicken and various fish dishes, including *lomi-lomi* salmon. Practically every type of island vegetable and fruit was available, as well as macadamia nuts. Caryn hesitated at a large bowl of purplish mass.

'Try just a little taste of that for starters,' Mike recommended. 'It's *poi*, a Hawaiian staple, sort of their version of mashed potatoes, made by pounding taro roots. Most Mainlanders aren't too fond of it.'

Caryn scarcely nibbled any of her food, but she nibbled even less at the *poi*. She didn't actively dislike it, but it seemed tasteless.

She waited until Mike polished off everything on his plate, then his second helping, before she prodded, 'Now will you please take me home?'

'But there'll be singing and dancing. It'll be fun.'

'Not for me. You don't seem to understand, Mike. I don't feel 100 percent welcome here.'

After trying to dissuade her, Mike

137

reluctantly agreed. Caryn found Kano eating with Hira and some others, and told him Mike was driving her home. He seemed surprised that she was leaving with Mike rather than Vance.

Caryn drew in her breath on discovering that she and Mike would have to walk by Vance.

'Leaving so soon?' The gray eyes seemed to interrogate her.

'Caryn is eager to get back,' Mike clarified cheerfully.

'I see. Well, goodbye, Mike. *Aloha*, Caryn.'

Unable to resist a quick glance back before they reached the parking area, Caryn saw Vance was still watching them.

During the hour's trip back she wondered why she couldn't be interested in Mike, except as a friend. Mike was attractive, personable, and considerate. He cared at least as much about her as Vance ever would. And Mike posed no danger of a permanent, someday painful, attachment.

Any inclinations Caryn might ever have developed in that direction were stifled by Mike's remarking, 'I don't know if you've seen her lately, but you met the other lady in my life the same day I met her at the Mid-Nite Inn in Kaunakakai.'

Caryn gasped, 'Tami?'

'Yes. Isn't she terrific? She hitched a ride back to Oahu with me that afternoon, and we've been seeing each other ever since, whenever our schedules work out so we're both in Honolulu at the same time. Tami's based there, but she spends a big chunk of each month flying all over the world.'

Well, hail Tami for one thing. She'd turned the cliché on the males: she had a boy in every port. But Caryn hated to see a great guy like Mike get hurt. Obviously, he didn't know about Tami's ongoing affair with Vance.

'It was Tami who invited me to the *luau* tonight. The anniversary couple are good friends of hers. But she got a last-minute call to sub for another stewardess on a flight to Hong Kong. I love these small community *luaus*, so I came on without her.'

Tami must have been aware of Vance's roving eye, and asked Mike to escort her in order to make Vance jealous, Caryn reasoned. She only wished Mike had clarified to Vance the source of his special invitation. But it was just as well, Caryn reminded herself for the hundredth time.

'Is it serious between you and Tami,' she probed casually, worrying if Mike was about to get hurt.

'No. Not yet. Maybe someday. Maybe never.'

Caryn wished she could adopt the same free attitudes toward relationships that Tami, Mike, and Vance all seemed to share.

She and Mike chatted for a while over iced tea in her cottage. When he left, they were silhouetted against the lamplight in the room as Mike bent and bestowed her a brushing kiss. 'Be seeing you, friend,' he murmured, and gave her hand a last squeeze.

Caryn watched Mike go, returning his final wave of farewell when he reached the end of the path.

She couldn't help looking toward the main house, though she saw only blackness. Then she thought she discerned movement on the second-floor balcony.

But, of course, it was her imagination. It was too dark to see anything.

CHAPTER EIGHT

Dawn was dappling the sky before Caryn finally captured a disturbed sleep. When she awoke after ten, the sun was beaming on WindsEnd, though gray clouds slouched bleakly against the hilltops.

I need to get away from here for a while, Caryn told herself during her shower. She decided to go as far as the road would take her, east to the Halawa Valley. She donned one of the two swimsuits she'd purchased in Honolulu, a not too skimpy bikini in lagoon turquoise, a color she'd figured would facilitate her blending with and feeling a part of the water to soothe away her problems, as well as a hue which complemented her skin and hair.

Over her bikini, she pulled on jeans, then tied the ends of a long red shirt around her midriff. Because she planned to make the hike to Moaula Falls, she put on socks and tennis shoes.

Low on groceries, she had nothing from which to concoct even a bare-bones picnic lunch. And there was no place to buy food between WindsEnd and the Halawa Valley.

Going to the kitchen door at the main house, she hoped not to encounter Vance. She could hear Hira humming a tune from the 1930s hit parade. Caryn knocked lightly.

Hira invited congenially, 'Caryn, come in.'

'I'd like to fix myself a picnic lunch. I'm going to Moaula Falls for the day, and I'm short of food at the cottage.'

'Of course,' Hira's amicable mood continued, 'only I will make it for you.' She peered intently at Caryn. 'I bet you haven't had a good breakfast either.'

'I'll grab an apple from the cottage to eat in the car.'

'I will cook you breakfast too.' Hira started toward the cabinets.

'No, please. I don't want you to go to any trouble.'

'Now don't act *lolo*.' Hira smilingly employed the Hawaiian word for 'stupid.' 'You need to start the day with a big meal.'

Caryn was starting the day near noon. But

141

she was ravenous, she realized, especially since she'd only picked at her portions of the feast last night. So she pitched in and helped Hira cook a huge omelet with ham, cheese, green pepper, mushrooms, and onion. Hira served it with sliced papaya and warm Molokai bread from the Kanemitsu Bakery, slathered with real butter and guava jam.

While Caryn stuffed herself, Hira put together an equally generous lunch of two shrimp-salad sandwiches, sliced mango in a plastic container, and home-baked brownies, then filled a small, lightweight thermos jug with iced tea. She included paper cups and napkins before relinquishing the sack to Caryn, who thanked her profusely.

Three square meals in a row could become habit-forming, Caryn thought ruefully as she headed the Toyota toward Highway 45.

Just when Caryn thought she couldn't take another mile of the zigzag, jigsaw road, it became smoothly paved—as if whatever bureaucrat allocated highway funds realized that tourists would reach the end of their patience before reaching the end of the road.

The scarlet cliffs and ebony rocks began to sport emerald ferns. Soon lush foliage edged the left side of the road, becoming ever more jungled as the asphalt trail curved down into the Halawa Valley.

Caryn strolled along the broad beach of blond sand, and watched a trio of young

Hawaiian surfers ride the high, fast waves. Skimming across the ocean looked like fun. Caryn wondered if she was too elderly to learn to 'hang ten,' the surfers' term for gripping the surfboard with their toes.

After dawdling a while she retrieved her lunch bag from the car, then ambled past a clear stream to the wide path leading gently upward for two miles to Moaula Falls. She stopped to admire one of the ubiquitous tiny white churches dotting Molokai, this one graced by a profusion of cultivated flowers and plants blending with the tropical surroundings.

The trail of hard-packed earth was damp from recent rains, and obviously would become a quagmire during one of Molokai's frequent deluges. She passed a scattering of small houses.

Eventually, she had to wade across a stream. In the middle, the fast-running water came nearly to her knees, and she reached the other side feeling like an intrepid, but soggy, adventurer.

The winds had been steadily increasing, but Caryn had become so accustomed to them that she hardly noticed. She estimated she was near Moaula when the sky supplied a major waterfall of its own.

At least there's no dangerous lightning, Caryn consoled herself as she found leaky shelter under the broad leaves of a wild banana tree.

The storm rampaged for half an hour before stopping as abruptly as it had begun. Undaunted, Caryn continued on to Moaula as the sun peeked tentatively around the corner of a cloud.

The sun was grinning broadly again when Caryn reached the waterfall, a slender 250-foot cascade shimmering into a crystal lagoon. Finding herself wishing Vance were here to share the beauty with her, Caryn scolded herself: *Lolo, lolo*—you've got to stop thinking about him.

Divesting herself of shoes and socks, Caryn poked the water with her big toe. Then she removed her shirt and jeans, and prepared to dive in.

'Wait, you can't go in there yet,' a disturbingly familiar male voice intruded.

As if conjured by her wishes, Vance stood at the edge of the trail, wet clothing defining every aspect of his marvelous physique—shirt clinging possessively to his expansive chest, jeans molding his muscular thighs.

Moments before, she'd been longing for him, but now she sallied sardonically, 'Sorry, I didn't know this was part of WindsEnd property.'

'It's not.' He advanced within a few feet of her, a smile toying with the corners of his mouth. 'But you wouldn't want to be done in by a lizard, would you?'

'A lizard?' Caryn recoiled as she scanned the

144

crystal water.

'Mo'o, the lizard god, who dwells in a cave at the bottom of the lagoon,' Vance explained the legend. 'You must check his mood before entering his domain by floating a ti leaf on the water. If it floats, so will you—but if it sinks . . .' Vance placed his hand over his heart and bowed his head.

Caryn couldn't help smiling as she glanced reflexively at the beautiful, huge, multicolored leaves of the ti plants festooning the landscape.

'How about ti for two? Mind if I join you?'

Caryn's clash between heart and head made her irascible. If only he'd leave her alone, maybe she'd have a chance of getting over him! 'As a matter of fact, I do mind. I came here today because I wanted to be alone and relax.'

'Be alone at one of Molokai's tourist attractions? It's just happenstance that no one else is here now. Can't you relax with me around?'

Absolutely not, Caryn thought. But she shrugged nonchalantly. 'I suppose. Suit yourself. It's a free lagoon.'

She dived into the water without waiting for the ti test. Might as well be bride of the lizard god as love slave to Vance Warner!

After swimming across the lagoon and halfway back again, Caryn turned onto her back and floated, pretending to have her eyes closed but actually peering through a tiny, and she hoped inconspicuous, slit—like she'd done as a teenager on Saturday mornings when she didn't want her father to make her get up.

Vance had remained at the edge of the pool, hands on his hips in perplexity. Now he began to strip slowly, and Caryn couldn't have taken her eyes, slits or otherwise, off Vance even if Mo'o had appeared at her side.

Vance leisurely unbuttoned his wet shirt, then peeled the fabric from his powerful tanned chest, revealing the furry mat of reddish brown hair. He tossed the shirt sideways, atop a rock, then unbuckled and slowly slithered his belt around his trim waist.

Vance unsnapped his jeans, then eased down the zipper. Caryn almost forgot to breathe, wondering if he planned on skinny-dipping, as Vance gradually stripped the denim from his firm flesh. His taut stomach was revealed, then...

He too was wearing a swimsuit beneath his jeans, red bikini trunks.

As he dived into the water, Caryn turned and swam toward the opposite edge, but Vance's expert strokes brought him even with her in seconds.

Placing one strong arm around her waist, he guided her upright. His silver eyes searched hers as they both treaded water, his arm continuing to hold her loosely, a not unwilling captive.

'Can't we pretend we're two tourists who just met here and decided to enjoy the afternoon together?' he asked softly.

'But you're not a tourist,' she teased.

'I'd say I'm at least as fascinated by the scenery as any other man would be.' Vance's eyes wandered in a visual caress along her face, along her pulsating throat, down to the swell of her breasts rising above her bikini top. In a voice husky with desire, he tried to make small talk: 'I see you haven't acquired much of a tan during your weeks in Hawaii.'

Her skin was not as lily white as when she'd arrived, but the sunbeams had dusted her only lightly. Her responding small talk sounded short and breathless. 'I don't tan much. In fact, I burn if I'm exposed too long.'

'Ummm'—his deep timbre caused her to vibrate within—'then we'll have to see that you're only exposed indoors.' His free hand moved to her shoulder. 'Maybe some of my tan could rub off on you...'

He pulled her close, displacing the water between them like a satin sheet drawn aside. His mouth descended on hers, and they drank of each other's sweetness. Caryn felt like she was drowning in desire...

Drowning. She was drowning! She and Vance both surfaced gasping for air.

'We forgot to swim,' he laughed.

'Mo'o almost got us,' she joked, as if to deny the effect had been totally Vance's.

She playfully splashed water in his face and paddled away, but he caught her by the ankle and effortlessly pulled her back. While she readied eagerly for another kiss, she received instead a reciprocal dash of water in her face.

Who was he? Today Caryn glimpsed the young boy, picturing Vance playing in this same place, in this manner, many years ago. Yet he was also the successful businessman; tough ranch manager; good friend to many on Molokai; the Champion Conclusion Jumper; and—she had no doubt—a tender, skilled, and consummate lover.

And who was she? The laughing girl frolicking in this lagoon today, or the sensible, mature lady? The tough construction superintendent, or the vulnerable female trying to fend off fears and doubts when she was alone? The sensuous woman, or the overgrown Girl Scout?

Molokai, the paradox paradise, Caryn repeated to herself.

After they cavorted and swam for some time, Vance hoisted himself out of the pool, then reached down to help her. His touch was electric—but then water conducts electricity, Caryn reminded herself austerely.

Vance caught her mane of tawny hair in his hands, guiding it back and gently squeezing out much of the residual lagoon.

Caryn said, 'I think we should go spread ourselves on the rocks to dry, like anhingas.'

'Anhingas?'

'Big birds that inhabit Florida. They're also

called snakebirds. They dive through the water to catch fish, then perch atop rocks and spread their wings wide,' Caryn gestured with her arms, 'until they dry out. They look like fowl Draculas with feathered capes.'

'You lived in Florida?'

'And most of the other fifty states.'

'Yes, you've been a lot of places. And I guess you have a lot more to go—a whole wide world awaiting.'

In that instant Caryn finally admitted to herself that she'd found the one and only place she'd ever want to remain for a lifetime—by Vance Warner's side, be it on Molokai or anyplace else. But he'd never offer her that option.

She started to clamber atop one of the huge boulders tossed like a giant's marbles at one side of the lagoon.

'Wait,' Vance interrupted. Grabbing up his shirt, he spread it over the boulder. 'My shirt's still wet,' he said as he lifted her up, his hands on her waist transmitting sparks throughout her being, 'but I wouldn't want that mean old rock to damage your soft skin.'

He added, 'I should be placing you on a pedestal instead of an ordinary rock.'

Caryn thrilled to his words as much as to his touch.

Then joking vanished as his left hand slowly slipped from her waist, down the slope of her hips, descending partway down her supple thigh, then moving atop her thigh. His hand massaged languidly in a small circle, fingers fanned, turning Caryn liquid. 'Such soft skin, like ivory velvet.'

He kissed her throat, at level with his lips, and she bent forward so their mouths could merge.

Again passion flooded through her. But she forced herself to remain aware of their surroundings. Laughing to cover her discomfort, she pulled away. 'Vance, we can't do anything here.'

He pulled back, teasing in a husky tone, 'I thought we were both outdoor types, in more ways than one.' His hands moved to her waist, holding her in a pulsating parenthesis. 'You're right, darling. I want everything to be perfect for our first time.'

Their first time?

No, there could never be a first time, because that would soon be followed by a last time, Caryn reminded herself sternly.

But she had the feeling that her heart wasn't listening. And the rest of her body was staging a total rebellion against her mind.

Retrieving Vance's shirt from the boulder, she commented, 'It looks like you got even more drenched than I did. You must have been out walking in the rain.'

'If Gene Kelly can dance in it, I can at least walk in it ... Besides, we shouldn't knock the rain. It brought me to you today.'

'What do you mean?'

'You'll see when we start back.'

'We can split the lunch I brought. Hira packed enough for two anyway.'

'Fine. But you'd better put some more clothes on first. You said you burn easily.'

His touch scorched her more than the sun ever could, Caryn mused as she returned to the spot where she'd left her clothing, and slithered her jeans up her long legs and over her hips.

'You know,' Vance said from some distance behind her, 'it isn't nearly as much fun to watch a woman dress as to watch a woman undress.'

Turning, Caryn saw Vance reclining under a palm, head back against his clasped hands, gazing at her. She threw her shirt at him in reprimand.

He threw the garment right back. 'Put it on, put it on,' he parodied the usual stripper encouragement of 'take it off' with a broad grin. 'I wouldn't want your skin to get any pinker than it already is.'

A good deal of her flush was temporary and attributable to Vance's steady stare, but she did have the beginnings of a mild sunburn too. She buttoned the red shirt all the way, and left it hanging loosely, fearing he would deem its previous midriff tie too provocative and they would once again become oblivious to any encroaching tourists.

'Aren't you going to dress too?' she asked as she picked up the lunch sack and sat down—

151

near him but not too close.

'I don't sunburn, remember. Besides, we match now,' he gestured to her bright shirt and his red swim trunks. 'Or will you admit that the sight of my near-naked body drives you wild?'

Her eyes traveled along his muscular legs and well-formed thighs, skipping self-consciously to his broad chest. 'Of course not,' she lied, pivoting her attention to opening the sack.

After they finished eating, Vance curved a long arm toward her. 'Come on over here and stretch out while we recuperate.'

She didn't doubt the recuperative powers of Vance's body, but resisted. 'We'd better be starting back.'

'In a little while. Afraid?' he pointed with his other hand to the available opening in his arm.

'Of course not.' Caryn rose and moved toward Vance, gingerly easing herself into the allocated space. His arm tightened reassuringly around her shoulder as she rested her head on his chest. She breathed in the male scent of him, fresh from the rain and the clear lagoon. Wrapping her right arm about his chest, she snuggled closer to the comforting warmth of his body.

Her eyes exercised a will of their own, determined to travel over his lean stomach and beyond. So she forced her eyes closed.

Some time passed before Vance kissed her eyes open. She stretched the length of her body languidly, enjoying the firmness of his form touching hers. 'I like having you wake up next to me,' Vance said.

'Ummm, so do I,' she replied in simple truth.

For moments she allowed herself to imagine the pleasure of waking up next to Vance every day. Then she came more fully awake and sat up. 'Gosh, I'm sorry I dozed off.'

His fingertips gently brushed the honey-colored strands away from her cheek. 'You must not have gotten much sleep last night either . . . I wouldn't have disturbed you, but we need to return to the cars before dark.'

Vance put on his still-damp jeans and shirt and dumped their picnic papers in the litter can provided. 'How about one for the road?' he said as he pulled her up off the ground with both arms in one long fluid motion until her figure was tight against his. Then he enfolded her and kissed her deeply.

They started hand in hand back down the trail, which was still quite muddy. Glad she'd worn washable tennis shoes, Caryn noted Vance had done the same.

Pink tinged the azure sky as they neared the stream. Soon a rainbow arched through the horizon. They stopped for a moment to fully admire it. 'A rainbow is a sign of good luck on Molokai,' Vance said.

He disappeared for a moment behind a clump of trees, then returned holding a coiled rope. 'Want me to lasso a rainbow for you, ma'am?'

She slid her arm around his waist, 'My own personal *paniolo*, huh? I think I'd rather keep you with me than have you off chasing rainbows. Let's leave it up there where it will bring good luck to everybody ... Why did you leave that rope there?'

'How do you know I didn't just hear it growing on a tree, and go pick it?'

Caryn laughed. 'Gee, I wish I'd brought my camera for a picture of that rare rope tree. Is there one nearby of the jumping variety as well as the lasso variety?'

'You'll see why we need it in just a minute.' Vance proceeded to secure one end around the trunk of a tree with silvery green leaves almost maple-shaped. 'This tree is a kukui. Its fruit has all sorts of uses. Since the kukui is Hawaii's state tree, it would never let us down.'

Caryn was confused by Vance's action before looking closely at the stream. It was more than twice as wide as earlier and appeared much deeper—and the current was very swift. 'Now I see what you're doing. Gosh, I wouldn't have been able to get back.'

'Worse yet, you might have tried, and *whoosh*, no more Caryn. On the other hand, it would provide a quicker way back to the ocean if you could manage to keep your head above water,' he kidded. 'I knew the clouds down this direction looked ready to burst when Hira mentioned you'd gone to Moaula, so I hurried to catch up with you.'

'You mean you crossed this stream—river—after it rained?'

'Darling, for you I would climb the highest mountain, swim the widest ocean,' Vance affected melodramatically.

'The highest mountain on Molokai isn't very high,' Caryn teased (though some of them were precipitously steep), 'but this "widest ocean" is something else.'

'To be honest, I have not yet performed that feat. I was past this point before the downpour. I considered tying the rope on both sides earlier, but I was afraid some tourist who wasn't in the best shape would try to use it to cross and would fail.'

'So that's why you were pretty sure we wouldn't be interrupted,' Caryn realized. 'No one else could get to Moaula after the storm. Will you be safe now, really?' Caryn worried as Vance stepped into the dangerously rushing water with the other end of the rope tied around his waist.

The water was lapping around Vance's waist seconds before the current yanked him off his feet. Caryn gasped as it jerked his body sideways, throwing him downstream, but in moments his powerful strokes transported him to the other side. She let out her breath in relief—she hadn't realized she'd been restraining it.

Vance removed the rope from his waist and

attached the end around a stubby palm.

Grasping the prickly rough fiber in both hands, Caryn started toward the torrent.

'Wait,' Vance ordered. 'I'm coming back to help you.'

'No, that would mean you'd have to cross three times. I'll be all right.' But he was already wading back in before she could protest further, one arm holding on to the rope while the other propelled him along.

He had Caryn wade ahead of him, using his body as a bulwark and extra support as long as possible. Then she pulled herself along with both hands as he provided extra propulsion from behind. The water was stunningly cold for the tropics.

As they both flopped down to rest a few minutes when they reached safety, Caryn said simply, 'Thank you.'

'At least we didn't go with the flow.'

'We seem to keep getting wet today, even though two times out of three weren't voluntary.'

Vance's fingers tangled affectionately in her hair. 'You've always been my rain girl.'

'I guess that makes you my rain beau,' Caryn punned impishly.

'And I hope this rain beau portends good luck too.'

Their lips sought each other simultaneously, kissing several times before once again hitting the trail.

The mud served as a constant reminder of the recent deluge. It squished around their every step, multiplying on their shoes and caking around the bottoms of their jeans until Caryn's legs seemed heavier each time she had to move forward.

At one point Caryn's feet betrayed her, sailing out from beneath her. Vance's arms caught her before she slid to the ground. 'We almost had a little slice of *déjà vu* there,' he kidded, then said softly in her ear as he continued to embrace her from behind, 'I hope tonight has a happier ending.'

Caryn couldn't let herself think beyond the current moment. She seemed incapable of making decisions, as if all her inhibitions and logic and good intentions had washed away in that stream.

Vance said as they neared their immediate destination: 'An extensive settlement, mostly taro farmers, once occupied the Halawa Valley. But the community was wiped out in 1946 by a tsunami—you might call it a tidal wave, but that's not technically correct. The early warning system worked, though. There were no casualties, but the residents watched their homes and fields being destroyed from atop that hill.' He gestured toward the point at which the road began its descent. 'Except for the few scattered homes along this trail, the area's never been resettled.'

When they reached the bottom of the valley,

sunset emblazoned the sky and gilded the wave crests with copper.

'I'm sure not driving back wearing all this mud,' Caryn declared, heading across the grassy expanse to the slower moving stream emptying into the ocean near the parking area.

'Sit down, and allow me,' Vance instructed. He knelt and removed her shoes and socks, then swiveled her lower legs into the water, rinsing as much muck as possible off her jeans, then rolling those up to gain entrée to her skin.

Gently, he sluiced the mud off the smooth flesh of her calves and ankles. Caryn quivered with delight under his touch. He tenderly massaged the stubborn remainder from her feet, giving careful attention to each toe. Caryn had never before considered the feet an erotic zone, but with Vance every millimeter of her body seemed to be one large and boundless erotic zone.

Finished, Vance swiveled her back around so that her soles rested on the grass. Then he raised each foot in turn, pressing his lips atop each one, as he said, 'Such pretty feet. If I didn't know they were just an extension of the rest of that gorgeous body, I'd say we should promote Molokai mud packs as a beauty aid.'

Then he unceremoniously swished his own feet in the stream after removing his shoes.

They divested their shoes of as much mud as possible, then walked barefooted to their cars. Caryn would have been tempted to chuck shoes and socks into the trash if shopping weren't so difficult on Molokai. Instead, she relegated them to the trunk of the Toyota.

'I hate to be away from you even for the hour to drive back.' Vance's hands rested on her shoulders.

'I know—me too...' She suggested mischievously, 'We could drive our cars bumper to bumper.'

'The road's dangerous enough without doing that,' he laughed. 'When we get to WindsEnd, darling, at the risk of sounding cliché, your place or my place?'

At the hesitant expression crossing her face, he added, 'For dinner, I mean.'

'Actually, it's a question of your place or your place, since the cottage is your property too,' she teased.

'The cottage's occupant is what I'd like to possess.' At the flicker of feminism simultaneously mingling with fear and desire in her eyes, he hastened to add, 'It's just a figure of speech. Besides, I know you'll never really belong to any place or any man.'

She found, incongruently, that she liked the idea of belonging to Vance—but only if he belonged to her too.

'Come to the main house as soon as we get back?' he asked. 'We can eat there.'

'I'll freshen up first, then I'll come.'

Still, he didn't release her from his embrace, and she didn't pull away.

Finally, he said, 'If I stand here and hold you as long as I want to, we'll never get back to WindsEnd.' He kissed her again. He slowly slid his hand down her arm, then caressingly across her palm in a lingering *aloha* until their fingertips parted reluctantly.

CHAPTER NINE

Caryn didn't dawdle when she reached her cottage. She was eager to be with Vance again.

And she didn't want to slow down. Didn't want to give herself time to think.

She showered quickly, and applied her makeup more carefully than usual. It seemed to her that appearing 'natural' required a lot more work than it ought to.

Encountering the small calendar open on her bureau reminded Caryn that today was her aunt's birthday. She vowed to make her traditional call from Vance's telephone as soon as she arrived at the main house. She'd had the department store mail her aunt's gifts the same day she'd bought them in Honolulu, well ahead of schedule.

As the hot breath of the blow-dryer fluffed up her already luxuriant hair, the tawny tresses flipped and bounced above her shoulders in anticipation of the evening.

Dressing up for Vance tonight meant

wearing the long, satiny multiblue abstract print, since she'd worn her other long dress last night.

In capricious competition with the island blossoms, Caryn misted on the only perfume she ever wore—the light, breezy fragrance of Prince Matchabelli's Wind Song.

Last, she put on strappy silver sandals and tossed a few essentials into a tiny silver evening bag.

Scrutinizing herself in the mirror, Caryn realized she looked radiant as a bride. But she wasn't a bride, and Vance had given her no indication that he ever wanted her to be.

Well, so what? She'd chosen singlehood a long time ago anyway. She was a vibrant, liberated woman who nonetheless sometimes felt adrift in the purgatory between old values and new lifestyles. A proposal would be merely an ego booster, she tried to convince herself, and compel her to rethink decisions she'd already finalized.

It was less complicated and much better this way—Vance's way. No long-term commitments, no being tied down. Free to go her own way and pursue her career.

But she realized now that her prior decisions had been based on insufficient data. She'd had no idea any man could set her aflame as Vance did with just a casual glance or a brushing touch.

She worked at evicting all such ponderances

from her mind as she hurried up the path to her beloved.

The strong wind was blowing directly *mauka*. Thus it seemed to urge and propel Caryn toward Vance, as if at last sanctioning their relationship.

Vance was pacing impatiently back and forth across the *lanai* spanning the front of his home. He'd changed into black slacks, with a raw silk shirt unbuttoned halfway down his chest.

He turned as one of the mounted electric lanterns caught and highlighted Caryn's features. They rushed toward each other.

His lips and tongue plundered her willing mouth with pent-up emotion as his hands explored the length of her back and hips. Their passions whirled as the winds swirled around them.

'I was afraid you'd change your mind and not come,' he murmured.

'No.' Caryn no longer had control over her mind. Only Vance, with his powerful magnetism over her, was determining her immediate future. She slid her hand upward along his cheek, but he grasped it and touched his lips to her palm.

He reached over and opened the front door, his other arm around her waist. 'Come into my parlor?'

'Are you sure you know who is the spider and who is the fly?' she teased.

'No, I'm not sure at all,' Vance responded with sudden solemnity. Then he regressed further to a tone of mild irritation: 'I wish you hadn't worn that dress.'

She was too surprised to be defensive. Instead, she apologized. 'I'm sorry you don't like it.'

'It's not the style—in fact, it's maddeningly becoming. Its history is what bothers me.'

'You mean you consider this a dress with a past?' she tried to joke.

'It's the same one you wore when you spent the night with Mike in Honolulu.'

Caryn's anger boiled within her. 'I only have two dresses suitable for seductions! I thought you invited me here for a tryst, not a trial!'

Now she was practically shouting. 'I don't owe you any explanations for anything, Mr Vance Warner. But for your information, Mike and I have never been more than friends. A friendly buss on the cheek has been the peak of our physical contact!'

Pivoting on her heel, she started to leave.

Vance's hands on her shoulders halted her exit. He pressed his body against hers from behind, then locked her more tightly in his embrace with fingers spread across her midriff and abdomen, transforming her to warm honey.

His breath titillated her ear as he murmured, 'Caryn, Caryn, I don't know why I brought that up. I know I have no claim on you, but you

163

don't understand how it rips me apart to think of Mike or any other man making love to you, or even touching you.'

She spiraled within the circle of his arms and said with lips upturned toward his, 'I do understand. I feel the same way thinking of you with another woman.' She didn't specify Tami.

He said hesitantly, 'I guess I should make a confession.'

Horrible 'confessions' caromed through Caryn's mind. He was married. He had seventeen children stashed in closets about the house. And besides he was engaged to Tami.

Vance continued haltingly, 'The day you were at the Mid-Nite Inn in Kaunakakai with Mike, it was I who had him called away—although I did pay his charter fee for three days to make up for it.'

Caryn laughed in delight that Vance had gone to so much trouble and expense to buy a couple of hours with her. 'Mike told me his eager customers never appeared—except by cashier's check.' Then she inserted with feigned casualness, 'By the way, Mike seems a bit hung up on Tami at the moment.'

'Really,' Vance didn't seem intrigued by that news, again bending his mouth to Caryn's and kissing her deeply.

Caryn's spirits soared. Vance must not care as much about Tami as he did about her, since the idea of Tami with Mike didn't upset him. Then she realized perhaps that only meant he was through using Tami as he'd someday be through with Caryn. His current interest might be due to the fact that Caryn was, thus far, an unconquered challenge.

Her brain tried to persuade her that she ought to leave this house right now and forget Vance Warner. But the sensations assailing and prevailing in every part of her body completely overwhelmed any wisp of logic.

'Oh, I almost forgot that I have to make a phone call tonight,' Caryn realized when Vance finally paused his foray against her sensibilities. Glancing at her watch, she calculated the time difference. 'I hope it isn't too late.' But her aunt was accustomed to spending the final hours of each day with a talk show or a vintage movie. 'I'll use the phone in the kitchen, and charge it to my credit card.'

Vance released her reluctantly. 'Talk fast.' Assuming Caryn wanted privacy, he didn't point out that there was a closer phone in the living room.

A correct assumption. She was debating telling her aunt about Vance during the course of their brief conversation, when her aunt said, 'You sound absolutely marvelous, dear—so bubbly and, I don't know, joyful.'

'The project's going well.'

'Is that all? I was hoping you'd met a special man.'

How her aunt's perception could travel thousands of miles along telephone signals was a mystery to Caryn, but she confided willingly, 'I have met a wonderful man.'

'That explains it,' her aunt laughed. 'When's the wedding?'

Never, as far as I know, Caryn thought. But verbally she lied, 'The relationship hasn't progressed far yet. You'll be the first to know if I have any big news.'

They chatted for a few more minutes before Caryn closed the conversation with 'Happy birthday again' and hurried back to Vance.

He was in the dining room when Caryn returned, lighting the duo of candles twisting within a golden base. In the flickering glow crystal goblets sparkled and expensive china gleamed alongside gold-plated dinnerware set at one end of the long, cherry-wood table.

As soon as he saw her, Vance held out his arms. Caryn returned to his embrace with an eagerness which frightened her. She wrapped her arms around him tightly, as if he might vanish.

'Business all finished?' he asked in a whisper.

'Uh-huh,' she mumbled against his warm neck, 'but it wasn't bu—'

His kiss cut her off, followed by two briefer ones, followed by a deep probe of her mouth with his tongue while his hands caressed her and pressed her to him. Eventually, Vance drew reluctantly away from her. 'I think I'd better pour the wine now.'

The crystal goblets converted to the color of

rich burgundy. Handing her one glass, with fingers lingering against hers, he offered a toast: 'To tonight.'

Not to the future. Just to tonight. That was obviously the extent of the future she could expect with Vance.

Caryn joined Vance in his toast, her eyes holding his.

She didn't know how many moments ticked past before he said, 'Hira left dinner for us.'

'Left? You mean she isn't here?'

'She's visiting friends in town for the night.'

Abruptly, that forced Caryn to try to rethink what she was doing, what she was going to do, here alone with Vance.

She said, 'Confident, weren't you?' But the question emerged as a sigh of desire rather than an indictment.

His words curled warmly around her as he answered softly, 'Just hopeful, darling.' After a pause he added, 'It was Hira's idea to spend the night in Kaunakakai, but I'll admit I didn't discourage her.' His eyes searched her face for any sign of censure, finding none.

Soon he said, 'I suppose if we don't heat up dinner now, we may never get around to eating.'

Eating. What was that? And who cared about such mundane activities. But Caryn's joking tone belied the deep emotions she was experiencing. 'Microwaving is my specialty.'

More than an hour passed in a blur after

that. Caryn was vaguely aware that they were doing things ordinary people do, although those things somehow seemed extraordinary tonight.

They laughed together as they retrieved Hira's carefully wrapped packages with toothpick flags planted in them, indicating the precise period for each to be reheated. Then they were eating beef Stroganoff with fluffy rice, broccoli, carrots, and salad.

Peripherally, Caryn was amazed that half their meals didn't wind up on their laps, because they scarcely took their eyes off of each other.

After dinner they walked into the darkened living room with arms about each other, carrying their wine glasses. Only the crescent of moon and the stars, visible through a wall of glass along the side, provided a muted platinum light.

Vance reclaimed the goblet from her hand before she could drink further, and intoxicated her instead with his kisses, enveloping her in his arms. She molded her pliant body against his firm form, clasping her arms around him tightly, traversing the planes and valleys of his back with her fingers through the silk that was so thin yet seemed such a barrier.

'Caryn, Caryn,' his whisper fanned her ear and spiraled through her being, 'stay with me tonight. Be mine, just for tonight.'

There it was again. For tonight. Only for

tonight. Or perhaps if she was lucky, for several more rendezvous before the resort was completed and she left Molokai.

Caryn stiffened in his arms, trying to resist. But his gentle kisses propelled all her other senses into oblivion, so that she was aware only of Vance and her throbbing need for him.

He was murmuring, 'Darling, I promise you a night so special that you'll always remember it, wherever you are.'

That was part of the problem. She could never forget Vance. Already she knew he would be a part of her thoughts and emotions forever. And that could only be worse in the future if they became physically intimate now.

A night that would be special for her, but not so special to him that he couldn't put her immediately out of his mind and his heart when she left Molokai, if not sooner.

She somehow found the mental strength to pull away from him. Trembling atop legs that seemed unwillingly to support her, she sat on the nearest piece of furniture, which happened to be a sofa.

'Vance, it won't work out,' she managed to say, attempting to maintain a calm voice.

He sat beside her, molding the side of his body against the side of hers, pressing his thigh against hers. His arm circled her waist, and she knew in that moment that she was his willing captive, that she'd never have the strength to break totally free of him.

169

His face, with his handsome features shadowed outlines in the darkness, hovered above hers. '"Work out"?' He repeated her last words in a low tone husky with emotion. 'I'm not talking about work, Caryn. I'm talking about pleasure, pure pleasure.'

His lips were tantalizing millimeters from hers as he whispered, 'If you wanted me even half as much as I want you...'

'I do,' she murmured, then realized that she might never say those words in the context of a marriage ceremony.

But did it matter, with half of all marriages ending in divorce anyway? Especially here on Molokai.

She should live for the here and now. Tonight. With Vance.

She had to have him, tonight. Even if for no longer than a single heartbeat.

She lifted her face, her mouth joining with his in a kiss that seemed to transcend time and place, catapulting her somewhere beyond that crescent of moon in the stratosphere.

He was pressing her against the cushions, angling her body beneath his...

She gently caught the lobe of his ear between her lips. It would be so easy to say what she wanted to say now. *I love you.*

She wanted to declare it a thousand times. Yet she couldn't say it once. She forced herself to hold back those three words, afraid he'd withdraw from her if what he considered a casual affair seemed to become too serious.

It would be simple to say it softly, into his ear resting so near her lips while his own lips were caressing her throat. *I love you.*

But instead she held it within herself, as she would soon be holding him within.

His body moving atop hers exerted a pressure more erotic than she had never known, as he locked her into his embrace while reaching to unfasten the zipper in back of her dress.

Caryn heard chimes, thinking all the old clichés about love must be true.

The bells rang out again.

'Just ignore the doorbell,' Vance muttered. 'Whoever it is will go away.'

But the visitor was persistent.

Vance seemed immune to the continued summons. But Caryn was distracted.

'You ought to answer that,' she inserted between kisses.

'If it's urgent, they'll come back tomorrow,' he mumbled. 'Or in a few days.'

'But what if it's an emergency on the ranch or at the project?' Her arms still clung to him even as her words urged him to leave.

Reluctantly, after a last kiss, he pulled back from her. 'Don't go away.' It was more of a plea than an order.

She heard him walk to the door, then heard the low murmur of unintelligible conversation.

As she drifted back down to earth, or at least

somewhere in the general vicinity, she glanced outside at the canopy of stars. Real stars. But no more real than the love she felt for Vance.

Only then did she become aware of an element which seemed determined to disburse those stars, to scatter them away from this room and from Caryn.

The wind shrieked outside, a cry of fury. It wailed down the fireplace and rattled at the windows as if trying to gain entry.

Vance was returning with quick strides. Turning toward him, Caryn held open her arms, wanting to hold him tightly, as if the wind might succeed and snatch him away.

But he seemed in no hurry to resume their embrace. Instead, he switched on the brightest light in the room.

Even blinking in the unaccustomed glare, Caryn could see that his silvery gaze had tarnished to black. Without his saying a word, she knew something was wrong.

He raked her with a look that laced contempt with desire, saying sarcastically, 'Your boyfriend's timing was a little off. A couple of more hours, and who knows what I might have signed, with such extra incentive.'

'What—' she started.

'He grasped her by the shoulders as she sat up. 'Or was his timing perfect? Are you promising me a bonus if I sign?' As she stood up, his fingers moved to the clasp of her zipper, with no gentleness this time. 'Maybe I should

172

look over what I'm about to pass up.'

Bringing her arms up and flinging them to each side, she broke his grasp. It wasn't difficult. She knew he'd had no intention of following through on his threat. 'Vance, I don't know what you're talking about,' she said in a voice which sounded surprisingly remote.

'Don't try to prolong this scene any more than necessary, Caryn, or we'll forget even discussing this. Your boyfriend arrived—'

'My boyfriend?' she interrupted.

'Stop the playacting. Sixty seconds. That's all the further we're going to talk. Your boyfriend, *Mike*, showed up—'

'Mike's not my boyfriend,' she interjected.

Vance continued in constrained fury, as if he hadn't heard her, '—with the special dispatch from your Jordan Nash. Coincidentally, the board of directors met yesterday and decided to raise their offer for the additional property for the golf course. Nash was sure that if he got new contracts to me immediately, I'd be ready to sign them tonight.'

Caryn tried to piece together Vance's reasonings. 'Jordan's been negotiating with you for extra land all along. I don't see why that has anything to do with us, one way or the other.'

'Caryn, Caryn,' Vance said with acid sarcasm, 'your portrayal of the innocent isn't at all convincing. I know that call you made

173

was the tip-off that I'd likely be very compliant tonight and agreeable to almost any offer Resorts Inc. made—along with certain direct offers from their superintendent.'

Every word he'd said since reentering this room was another dagger plunged into Caryn's heart. She swallowed hard, willing the tears to evaporate in the wells of her eyes before they could escape. A few defied her.

'Tears, Caryn? Nice touch. Unfortunately for you, I'm not a man who falls apart at the sight of a woman's makeup streaking.'

Caryn's voice sounded calmer than she felt as she tried to conceal the pain and shame turmoiling within her. 'It doesn't matter, Vance. I'll leave in a minute, and I'll never be back. Other than residing in the cottage, *per our contract*, I won't set foot on Warner property, and I don't want you trespassing on the resort property.'

'Fine,' he started toward the door.

'Darn you,' she summoned him back. 'I listened to your rantings. Now you hear me out.'

He halted, but didn't look at her.

'You're wrong about *everything*. Never has one man been so wrong about so much. I didn't know Jordan was making you a new offer; I'm not involved in acquisitions. The telephone call was to wish my aunt a happy birthday.' Then her voice cracked treacherously, out of control: 'I don't know how you could think I'd make love to you or any other man for a crummy piece of property—'

'About that crummy piece of property—your boyfriend's making himself a sandwich in the kitchen while he follows Nash's orders to wait for my response. Nash is hoping I'll return signed contracts. I've told him all along that I won't sell more land unless and until I'm financially forced to do so, which I hope will be never again, but that if that circumstance occurred, I'd sell to him.'

Vance had turned, and his eyes flung poisonous silver darts at Caryn. 'The response Nash is getting from me won't be the one he's anticipating. I'm writing that I will never sell to Resorts Inc. under any circumstances, that if such a time should come, I'll sell to anybody *but* Resorts Inc. I won't deal with a company that employs such seedy tactics.'

Vance sprang from the room like an enraged tiger.

Caryn felt empty, so incredibly empty. At first she could hardly bring herself to move, then realized she wanted to get out of Vance's house, out of his life, as soon as possible.

She rushed to the refuge of her cottage. The cheery yellow interior seemed to mock her.

She stripped off her clothing even faster than she'd put it on, and headed for the shower, anxious to wash away the touch and the memory of Vance Warner.

But it wasn't to be, darn him. It wasn't to be.

Her rivers of tears mingled with the spray of the shower as moment after moment fled by.

As she toweled the rest of her body dry, she managed to stop crying too. There would be no more tears ever, she determined—not for Vance, not for any man.

Her future remained where it always had been, in her career.

CHAPTER TEN

Making decisions and vows was one thing. Putting them into practice was another.

So she'd had one sleepless night. That was the last time she'd lose sleep over any man.

Caryn dressed for work in her usual cotton shirt and jeans. Automatically, she plunked her hard hat over her honey-colored hair before leaving the cottage.

Flinging open the door, Caryn was astounded to see Vance poised outside, fist raised.

Involuntarily, she drew back.

'I was just getting ready to knock,' he said.

'What are you doing here? Come to burn the witch at the stake?'

The silver eyes looked haunted. 'I came to say I'm sorry, Caryn.'

The word had become easier for him to say, yet had less meaning.

He forced a hopefully irresistible half smile as he reached for her hand. 'Contrary to last decade's pop philosophy, I guess love means always having to say you're sorry.'

Love. Funny that the first time he mentioned love, it was in such a context. And as meaningless as his apology. Caryn jerked her hand away.

'You'll pardon if poor dense me,' she said caustically, 'inquires into the reason for such a humble apology from such a perfect man.'

'Okay, Caryn. I have that coming, and more. I'll listen to any tongue-lashing you want to give me. You can even punch me out if it will make you feel better.'

'Well, you seem determined to prolong this scene unnecessarily,' she parroted. 'You have sixty seconds to explain, or—' She made as if to leave.

'Okay, okay. I said I'm sorry. I couldn't mean it more.' He tried to place his hands on her shoulders, but she shrugged them off. 'Mike was chattering away when I went back to the kitchen. I was barely listening, until he mentioned that this dispatch envelope was supposed to be delivered to me yesterday afternoon, but that he couldn't fly to Molokai because of the weather. Besides the rain, the winds were too treacherous. In fact, he had trouble landing after he got this far last night.'

'So?' She flung the single syllable like a gauntlet.

'So you couldn't have known earlier that we'd be together last night.'

'So?' Another gauntlet, even though she continued to comprehend his meaning.

Reaching out to embrace her, anticipating her happy response, Vance finished lightly, 'So forgive me?'

'No.' She stiffened her body and drew back.

For once, it was he who looked stunned and dismayed. 'What—'

'I said no. I don't forgive you. And I won't forget. Like I said earlier, I don't ever want to see you again.'

'You've got a hard head under that hard hat, lady,' he tried to kid her into a more receptive mood.

'Neither are as hard as the heart that beats beneath those cool tropical shirts you wear.'

'Caryn, it's understandable that you're upset. It was all my fault. But don't you think we should at least talk this over, after what we were to each other last night—'

'After what we were to each other last night, you accused me of using my body as a cheap negotiating tool. But then that wasn't too original, considering that you'd previously accused me of getting this job by sleeping with my boss. What did you think a high-rolling hooker like me was getting in return for sleeping with Mike, which you also assumed?'

Vance looked as defeated now as Caryn had been, still was. 'Caryn, I don't know what else I can do except apologize.'

He grasped her more firmly by the shoulders, but refusing to acknowledge the resulting sensations, she steeled herself to his touch.

Vance studied his foot nudging the red earth for a second before lifting his eyes directly into hers and saying softly, 'Caryn, I love you.'

Oh God. Why couldn't he have said that last night when she needed so badly to hear it, when she longed to cry out that same phrase in return? What difference did it make now anyway?

'I don't think you know the meaning of the word, any more than you seem to know me.'

Gradually, his hands withdrew from her shoulders as disbelief flooded his silver eyes, spilling over the rest of his features—oh, those wonderfully handsome, chiseled features.

But Caryn forced herself to continue: 'You're always eager to believe the worst about me. You're always fabricating some awful version of me in your own mind. A man who loved me would stand by me, no matter what. He'd take my word over anybody else's about anything. Even if I did make a mistake, he'd help me and see me through it. And if love isn't like that, I don't want it anyway.'

'Caryn, I'll say it again,' he pleaded his case with unaccustomed humility. 'I've been a complete idiot, a total fool. But I do love you.'

'That's your problem.'

Caryn willed herself into a walking statue of stone as she brushed past him and continued toward the site. She hoped he was feeling even a fraction of the pain that he'd caused her.

She willed the suspension of all her senses, all her feelings. She didn't smell the fragrant plumeria or pikake, nor the fresh sea air. She didn't hear the symphony of birdsongs. She didn't see the azure waves caressing the golden sands. She didn't feel the wind rifle her hair and palpate across her face.

Past quitting time that same afternoon Caryn and Kano were walking across the site comparing notes and comments when a gale suddenly swooped upon them.

'Darned balmy breezes,' Caryn mumbled irascibly as they intensified.

In moments the wind escalated to more than fifty miles per hour. Caryn and Kano realized simultaneously that they'd better find safe shelter.

'The field office might blow over.' Kano echoed Caryn's thoughts about the nearest building. Its lightweight modular structure might not withstand the onslaught.

The workers' modular housing probably would remain upright, with several units locked together, but was too far away. Caryn noted a scattering of employees heading inside. Her cottage was even more distant.

Tall palms bent low in surrender and supplication as Caryn and Kano debated their choices. They were closest to Building No. 3, but it offered the least protection, with only the frame and one exterior wall completed.

'We'll head for No. 2.' Kano designated the middle building as they started to run.

'No, the roof's only half on. It might go,' Caryn shouted, her words almost snatched away before they could reach Kano's ears. 'We'll have to try to make No. 1.' Building No. 1 was farthest away but the most completed.

They sprinted across the grounds, Caryn noting that Kano hadn't lost much of his speed as quarterback at the University of Hawaii more than forty years ago. She was amazed a man of his bulk could move so fast, and felt he might even be holding back so as not to outdistance her.

As they passed No. 2, the wind ripped the tarpaulin off the stack of gypsum board waiting in readiness for the interior finishing.

'Oh no,' Caryn yelled. 'Watch out. Go on ahead of me. I'll make it.'

As Caryn had feared, the gale began to peel the heavy four-by-eight-foot white boards rapidly one by one off the stack, as if it was nothing more than a flimsy deck of cards. Gusts filled the five-eighths-inch-thick boards, curving them almost into semicircles.

In seconds several traveled through the air above the grounds, like billowing sails of phantom ships piloted by the spirits of the winds.

'My gosh,' Kano puffed, 'those boards weigh more than forty pounds each.'

Yes. And if one crashed down on them...

Caryn halted just in time to avoid one that came skirring in front of her.

Another poised overhead as Caryn and Kano finally reached a doorway in Building No. 1. The board careened to the ground a millisecond after the two had stepped safely inside.

Caryn turned in the open doorway to determine the source of the next sound, a thundering, ripping noise. She saw the roof was indeed being torn off Building No. 2, and new missiles filled the air, some colliding with the billowing sails of gypsum board.

'Come on. We'd better get further inside in case the windows blow,' Kano urged.

Caryn was not ready to surrender totally. 'At least maybe we can save the windows in this one unit,' she resolved, 'if we open them all to equalize the pressure.' She began by pushing completely open the sliding door through which they'd entered.

Since it was a middle apartment, Kano had only to open the windows at the back.

Then they sat on the floor in the cubicle which would be completed as the bathroom, the only area with all interior walls and no windows.

The winds rampaged through the other rooms, as if seeking their prey.

'I've seldom seen it like this in all my years on Molokai,' Kano commented.

Stop this siege, Caryn wanted to yell at the blasts of air. You had already won. I know Vance can never be mine. I'm leaving here as soon as this job's done; I wish I could go sooner. All your damage to the construction is only prolonging my stay.

'Dumb wind,' Caryn muttered under her breath, then said louder to Kano, 'The wind is *lolo*, *pupule*—stupid, crazy.' Then she realized she was beginning to sound a little *pupule* herself.

If Vance had complied with her ban from this property, at least he was spared from the current havoc. She hoped he was safe somewhere. No, she really was going to go *pupule* if she allowed herself to think of him.

'The wind isn't usually nearly so bad,' Kano repeated and comforted. 'I can show you how to capture a bit of it and make it carry you on its wings.'

She smiled. 'I'd be afraid of a crash landing.'

'No, really. I will show you. Perhaps next Sunday if the breezes are normal ... Oh, wait, Now I am *lolo*.' He pretended to smack his forehead with the heel of his hand. 'You probably want to spend your Sundays with Mr Warner.'

'No, Kano. Never on Sunday. Never anytime. That's all over, kaput.'

'Funny, isn't it, the different languages. In

German and now in English too, "kaput" means "finished, done for." The similar word in Hawaiian, *kapu*, means "forbidden, never allowed to get started."'

Yes. Anything between her and Vance seemed always to have been *kapu*, which had led to kaput.

'Don't you want to spend Sundays with Hira?' Caryn rerouted the conversation.

'That is *kapu* by Hira,' Kano said sadly.

'Do you feel like talking about it?' Caryn offered in sympathy and empathy.

'Hira is a wonderful woman. You must realize how much she's accomplished, how many changes she's adapted to in her lifetime, since she arrived in Hawaii a young and frightened mail-order bride decades ago.'

'Decades ago? I didn't think Hira was that old.'

'She is nearly the same age as me. But you're right. She has retained much of her youth and beauty.'

Kano clasped and unclasped his huge bronze hands before continuing. 'The husband chosen in advance for her was a very old man. He died two days after the wedding without ever consummating the marriage.

'That was when I first knew her. We worked in the same pineapple fields, both of us just teenagers. Japanese women were much in demand as wives for the immigrant Japanese workers, particularly the older ones who had fulfilled their family duties by sending money home for many years and who could then afford to support a wife.'

'That's an awful system, first unfair to the man who couldn't marry while he was young, then even more unfair to a teenage girl who was forced to marry him.'

'On the whole, the system worked very well for almost everyone. And history still repeats itself, only now it is the Filipino immigrants following that path.'

Caryn thought of her two Filipino women employees. She'd wondered why their husbands were so much older.

'Hira, being so beautiful, had many choices for her next husband. Though I thought she loved me even then, I was not quite ready for a wife. Since her relatives were all still in Japan, Hira was even allowed a little say in the selection of her next husband.

'He was a fine man, not yet forty. They were married a month after Pearl Harbor. Perhaps she felt she needed the protection of a husband particularly then, even though Hawaii fortunately did not treat its Japanese-Americans so deplorably as the Mainland did, herding them into prison camps.' He spit out the last phrase.

'Hira's second husband was well-educated, and very brave. He became a lieutenant in the Nisei Brigade, the unit comprised of Japanese-Americans. Ironically, many of them were

185

fighting for the same country that was illegally and unjustifiably incarcerating their families. The Nisei Brigade was the most decorated unit in all the U.S. military during World War II, and suffered the highest percentage of casualties. Her husband never returned. He died in Germany during the last months of the war. Actually, they'd had very little time together.'

'How sad,' Caryn commented, engrossed in Kano's story.

'With a slight widow's benefit, Hira didn't have to remarry right away, though the pressure on her to do so was great. I returned from the war then, and we thought at last the time was right to pursue our love. I courted her in the old ways, the romantic, unrushed ways. I asked her to marry me. But the Japanese-American community, particularly her second husband's relatives and friends, exerted influence on her. They convinced her that she owed it to her husband's memory to marry another Japanese-American.'

Memories drifted in his dark eyes. 'Hawaii has always been considered the great melting pot, with many, many intermarriages among all nationalities. But this one was not to be. Hira was unable to withstand the pressure.'

He hastened to defend: 'Oh, like I told you before, she is an admirable woman. To have arrived in a strange country not speaking one word of the language and have made any life

186

for herself at all was an achievement in itself, particularly in view of the cloistered rearing and extremely restrained status of women in Japan at that time.'

'Yes, of course, a very great accomplishment,' Caryn agreed.

'Hira's third husband was a cousin of her second, and closer to Hira's age. He was one of the survivors of the Nisei Brigade. I think he really cared for her, and I believe she came to love him. They had three children, as you probably know.'

'I didn't know,' Caryn said, puzzled.

'I left that plantation then, and worked at creating much of the urban sprawl that is now Honolulu. I didn't see Hira again until that evening at Melveen Leed's show.'

'But Hira is a widow again now, isn't she?'

'Yes, a three-time widow afraid to make another change in her life. There would be little if any pressure against us from the general community, but she is afraid her family might disapprove. Her family is all she has to show for over half a century of living. She says she's too old to fight it.'

Caryn reached over and covered part of Kano's huge hand with her own. 'You're worth fighting for, Kano. I think Hira will realize that.'

CHAPTER ELEVEN

Always the professional, Caryn threw herself even more into her work. And now was a good time for that, since the work crews had to devote more than two days to cleaning up the site after the violent windstorm.

Where windows had blown out in some of the apartments in Building No. 1, a power vacuum was used to extricate every bit of glass from the dirt outside as well as from the interiors. Shingles, gypsum board, and miscellany were picked up and either scrapped or saved, while necessary replacement materials were rushed from Honolulu.

The field office became upright once again after having been topsy-turvied onto its side. Fortunately, the telephone line had remained connected, so Caryn didn't have to make her business calls from Vance's house.

Each night Caryn stood alone and exhausted in her darkened cottage looking toward the balcony of the main house, toward Vance's room. She sometimes imagined that she saw a shadow moving in the blackness.

But she knew that was all it was. Imagining, wishing that he was experiencing the same agony.

One thing she did know for a fact: Vance Warner was a proud man. He had humbled himself to Caryn once. Having been rejected, he would never do so again.

If there was to be a next move, it would have to be hers. A step she couldn't, shouldn't, take.

She worked all day on Saturday. Then she and Kano tried to console each other on Sunday. As promised, on a beach to the west, Kano showed her how to ride the wind. Windsurfing was the more popular term, although the sport was technically called board sailing.

Kano had borrowed an extra sailboard from a woman friend. He explained that windsurfing, based more on responsiveness and agility than on strength, was well suited to women.

Caryn learned to balance herself on a board, two feet wide and eleven feet long, while maneuvering a fourteen foot sail attached by a swiveling rubber joint. After a few hours she had acquired the rudimentary skills and was enjoying herself, although the capricious zephyrs dumped her into the ocean many times.

Her first sound sleep in a week finally followed on Sunday night, since she was sufficiently physically fatigued to counterbalance the emotional tension plaguing her for the prior six nights.

The drone of a light aircraft awakened her early Monday morning. Later, leaving for work, she noticed Tami in the briefest of bikinis, preparing to sun herself on the upstairs *lanai* at Vance's house.

So Vance loved Caryn. Big joke. She shouldn't have let those words haunt her for the last week. She'd been right when she'd told Vance that he didn't know the meaning of the word 'love.'

That night was again sleepless, though. In her dark cottage Caryn paced in front of her windows for hours, looking out into the inkiness that eclipsed her view of Vance's house in general, his bedroom in particular—where there were no lights.

Then she tossed and turned in her bed—her bed that seemed so incredibly empty, as empty as she felt—until finally deciding more physical exercise like yesterday would tire her so much that sleep would triumph.

Her digital travel alarm showed 2 A.M. when she slipped a caftan over her bare skin and left the cottage. A small flashlight aided her along the route to the beach. Then she extinguished its beam since the strand of vanilla sand had no hazards and was dimly illumined by a sliver of moon. The only thing visible was frothy white scalloping atop the raven waves nuzzling the shore.

She walked the beach slowly, more like a somnambulist than an insomniac, kicking at the sand with her toes.

Suddenly, a large figure of a man loomed in front of her. She stifled a reflexive scream, relegating it to a startled gasp.

'Caryn? What are you doing out here this time of night?' The timbre of that voice was enough to set her shaking.

'Vance, what are *you* doing here?' she answered with another question, straining inconspicuously to see if Tami was close behind.

'Excuse me,' he said sardonically, 'I must have strayed onto Resorts Inc. property.'

'You know that all beaches in Hawaii are legally public ... Besides, you know I didn't mean it when I said you could never set foot on company land.'

'Was there anything else you said that you didn't mean?'

Yes, every pore of her body screamed in unison. I want to see you again, and again and again and again. But her brain asked how dare he confront her like this with his mistress stashed less than half a mile away. She responded to his opening with silence.

Returning that cacophonous silence, Vance pivoted and strode away, in a heartbeat swallowed up by the night.

Lingering on the beach, Caryn felt bereft, as if she existed in a total void, oblivious to everything. At last resurrecting a little of herself, she became vaguely aware of her surroundings.

She listened to the song of the surf, the rhythmic chant of the waves rushing to meet their destiny on the shore.

It was the cadence of endless heaven, endless earth, endless time, endless love. A lament of love *kapu*.

*   *   *

Caryn remained excruciatingly aware of Tami's presence at WindsEnd for the next few days, so she tried to keep herself busy. When dedication at the office failed her, she left in the late afternoons. A couple of evenings she drove all the way into Kaunakakai—although everything was closed except the hotels and small eateries—and didn't return until after midnight, totally fatigued. The smooth skin beneath her eyes began to show the shadows of strain, both emotional and physical.

Love. First Vance wouldn't say the word. And he might as well never have, since it was meaningless to him.

Seeing his plane return one afternoon, she could no longer resist a confrontation. She intended to tell Vance Warner in no uncertain terms exactly what she thought of him!

She found him in the hangar, tying down the Beechcraft. Her first response on seeing him was a flood of emotion and desire. She noticed that even in profile he appeared tired and strained too, and that she wasn't the only one with eyes bordered by dark shadows.

She had held back her words too long so, like

an arrow released from the tension of a tightly drawn bow, they whizzed toward the unsuspecting target. 'How dare you say you love me!'

'Caryn?' His lips caressed her name as he turned toward her, before he recoiled for a normal response. Then he answered quietly, 'I dared to say I love you because I do. But don't worry. I'll never bother you by saying it again.'

'How can you say it now, with your mistress staying at the main house?' she shouted at him.

'My mistress?' He looked puzzled for a second before realizing, 'You mean Tami?'

'You have more than one?'

Anger tightened his features. 'I have none at the moment. But I may remedy that soon. As for Tami, she's here to visit her mother.'

Caryn was a bit uncertain for the first time. But she couldn't quite let go of her assumption. 'Sure. And all the hotels were full, so she had to stay at WindsEnd.'

Vance's answer matched her loud, irritated tone. 'Why should Tami stay at a hotel more than an hour's drive away when we have plenty of rooms right here? She'd spend half her time driving instead of visiting Hira.'

Slowly, the dawn of recognition forced through the dark tortures of Caryn's mind. 'Hira is Tami's mother?'

Vance's voice grew calmer. 'You didn't know that?'

'No. No one ever mentioned it.'

He was astounded at the coincidence of her not knowing. 'I guess Tami never happened to address her as "Mother" in your presence.'

Caryn knew she must look as mortified as she felt.

After a long pause Vance said, 'I'm sorry for what you must have gone through. I know what I've gone through in misjudging you. But maybe it's just as well this happened.'

'Why?' she managed to ask.

'Because now I've been unseated as the Champion Conclusion Jumper.'

When her expression of unhappiness continued, he added with an undertone of desperation, 'Is having a defense mechanism in common enough to build a relationship?'

She swallowed hard, then sighed deeply. 'No. We don't have enough foundation. I guess—' She choked back a cry that threatened to wrench from deep within her soul. 'I guess it's always been hopeless for us. I'll be leaving soon.'

His features were openly distraught, and she knew her own face mirrored that torment. Bowing her head in defeat, she mumbled, 'I'm sorry I misunderstood about you and Tami. I'll always remember you, Vance. But there can't be anything more between us.'

She felt his eyes on her as she turned and left.

*   *   *

She was walking toward her cottage after five o'clock a couple of afternoons later when she saw Tami waiting in front. For a split second, since Tami hadn't noticed her yet, Caryn wanted to turn and run away. You are acting *pupule*, Caryn told herself, resolutely proceeding toward her door.

Despite Vance's reassurances, Caryn had noted the affection in Tami's eyes when she looked at him, even if he didn't return it. Was this to be the showdown? Molokai isn't big enough for both of us? Get off this island by sundown, or else? Had Tami come to warn her away from Vance or Mike or, piggishly, both?

'*Aloha*,' Tami greeted congenially as Caryn approached. Her wispy sundress in golden print flattered her amber skin. Caryn felt slovenly in her work-soiled jeans and shirt. 'You're a busy lady. I've been trying to see you for the last couple of days. I was afraid I'd miss you before I leave in the morning.'

'Leaving so soon?' Caryn forced herself to reply lightly.

'I've been here since Monday. This was a much longer stay than usual.'

How well Caryn knew that. 'Come on in.'

Tami helped herself to a chair, chattering small talk while Caryn plunked her hard hat down on the table, chunked ice into two glasses, and splashed in Dr Pepper. Tami got down to business when Caryn was seated too.

'I want to talk to you about Vance.'

195

'There's nothing to discuss.'

'I'm sorry to be pushy, Caryn, but I think there is.'

Caryn swiggled her Dr Pepper, the ice cubes clashing against the glass. 'He's all yours, Tami.'

'All mine?' Tami looked astonished before smiling, 'No, you've got it wrong. He's all yours. I just don't understand why you don't want him, what's wrong between you two?'

Caryn's shock was evident. 'I don't know what you mean. Aren't you in love with Vance?'

Tami shrugged good-naturedly. 'I was in love with Vance Warner from the time I was three years old. I started trying to seduce him when I was thirteen, but he was twenty and thought I was a scrawny, pesky kid. He was the first love. I'd never planned it any other way.'

Then it was Tami's turn to toy with the liquid in her glass before she continued, seeming willing to be totally open with Caryn. 'I had just graduated from the University of Hawaii in Honolulu and was accepted for flight-attendant training before Vance finally succumbed. We saw each other only for a few months and only in Honolulu. Vance would never make love to me at WindsEnd out of respect for my mother.'

'But you come here now only to see your mother?'

'Not totally, to tell the truth. Sometimes my

mother was more of an excuse than the actual motivation for my visits.'

'But you said Vance wouldn't make love to you at WindsEnd.'

'Vance and I haven't been involved for almost two years, since I turned down his proposal.' Noting Caryn's look of incredulity, Tami continued, 'I think Vance decided, incorrectly, that he had taken advantage of me, that he should make an honest woman out of me. So he proposed finally. But by then I'd found a new love—travel. Molokai is so small, so secluded. When I started flying with TransGlobal, I had Paris, Hong Kong, Bangkok, Amsterdam—the whole world before me.'

Tami gazed retrospectively into the cold fireplace before proceeding. 'I've known Vance all my life, and I've sensed the depth of his feelings for you every time I've seen you together, growing ever stronger. Now I'm aware of those feelings even though you're apart.'

'You and Vance may get back together one of these days,' Caryn ventured.

'No, I used to think that, but not anymore. I used to think that I could have my fill of the rest of the world, then someday when I was ready come back to Molokai and to Vance. In my fantasy he'd always be waiting for me. But that changed the day I turned down his proposal. The day you arrived on Molokai, I began to feel less guilty about my decision.'

'If Vance feels anything for me,' Caryn insisted as she launched herself out of the chair and began pacing the floor, 'it's only the physical longings of a man who's been alone on an island for two years.'

'You must know you're wrong about that. Vance could have flown to me in Honolulu anytime I was there, until recently, not to mention taking his pick from dozens of women on five islands any time he wanted to.'

Caryn continued to pace, unconsciously clenching and unclenching her hands, biting on her lip.

'Please trust me enough to talk to me about it,' Tami prodded. 'I want to help.'

'I know you do, and I thank you for coming,' Caryn halted for a moment and offered a weak smile. 'But you don't understand.'

'I want to.'

'Vance doesn't love me, not really. He concocts the most awful versions of me in his own mind, images that no one could have of someone he loved.'

'For instance,' Tami prompted.

'First he accused me of getting my job by sleeping with my boss, who's an old friend of my father's. Then he jumped to the conclusion that Mike was my lover.' She hastened to add, 'Mike and I have never been more than casual friends.'

Tami looked relieved to hear that. Her head

of lustrous black hair bobbed up and down in empathy.

'The worst was...' Caryn hesitated, but responded to Tami's open look and sharing of confidences. She swallowed hard before proceeding. 'We almost spent one night together, and he accused me of using my body to persuade him to sell additional land to my company.'

Tami didn't look astonished, as Caryn had expected. Instead she said, 'Don't you see what Vance was doing? He was trying to defend himself against you. If he could make himself believe you were in some way a bad person, even a less than perfect person, he subconsciously hoped that it would ease his heartbreak if and when you left Molokai and him.'

'But he's never asked me to stay, never indicated in any way that he wants me to.'

'Of course not. He's a proud man, and he's afraid you'll refuse. Or, worse yet, that you'll stay for a while, then he'll be even more alone when you do go.'

Caryn was beginning to comprehend Tami's line of reasoning. 'The way his mother left his father.'

'Yes. The way dozens of women have left Molokai—Kano's wife, for example. Rock fever, they call it—the inability to adjust to life isolated by the sea, with no place to go but around in circles—and on Molokai you can't do even that. I was born to it, but I left. In fact, I think Vance might have proposed to me because he figured at least I was accustomed to Molokai. But while I love Molokai and WindsEnd—and Vance, though not with the passion of my youth—'

Caryn had to grin since Tami couldn't be more than twenty-five.

'—even I wouldn't stay here.'

'I might be able to adjust to living on Molokai, although it wouldn't be easy.' Caryn added honestly, 'Right now I feel like I'd happily reside in an igloo in the frozen Arctic if I could be with Vance.'

'The Arctic probably wouldn't be frozen too long in that case,' Tami quipped.

Caryn couldn't manage even to tilt up her lips at Tami's remark, continuing forlornly, 'But it wouldn't work. I couldn't live with his perpetual suspicions, his constantly waiting for me to leave him, trying to prepare himself for it. The adjustments in general lifestyle and marriage would be difficult enough with Vance's full support and trust. Without that I wouldn't even want to try.'

'It definitely takes two. But remember, you made incorrect assumptions about Vance too—and about me.'

'That's true.' But as they'd already determined, similar defense mechanisms were insufficient grounds for marriage. 'I'm sorry,' Caryn offered belatedly. 'I've been very unfair to you.'

'I forgive you. I didn't even know what you were thinking until now. But you've also been unfair to Vance.'

'Yes.' Caryn's facial expression and tone were dolefully pensive. 'Maybe we're just two loners destined to remain alone.'

Tami seemed to reflect some of the melancholy that Caryn was feeling. 'Please think about it some more. Don't make a decision you'll always regret.'

'I'm afraid I'd have to live with regret either way. At least if I leave, I'll have a chance to get over him someday.'

'Don't count on it,' Tami discouraged.

Caryn reached out and touched Tami's hand. 'Thank you for coming. I'm glad I understand the circumstances now, even if they can't be changed. But please let's talk about something else. What about Kano and Hira?'

'What about them?' Tami responded eagerly. 'Vibes of romance are all over this end of the island, but I haven't been able to pry any information out of my mother.'

Hoping that she wasn't betraying Kano's confidence, or that if she was, it was for a good cause, Caryn related what Kano had told her.

Tami clapped her hands together in delight when Caryn finished. 'That's terrific!' Then she added as an afterthought: 'Poor mother. Imagine thinking her children would object to her finding happiness with Kano. I suppose she was afraid we'd think her unfaithful to our father's memory. I'll set her straight immediately, and tell my brothers to do the same. In fact, my older brother, who's a medical student at the University of California in Los Angeles, is ready to announce his engagement to a pretty Japanese-American nurse who grew up on the Mainland.'

Tami chattered on exuberantly. 'My younger brother is a sophomore at the University of Colorado. He'll be excited for her too. Vance paid for college for all of us, you know—no, of course, you didn't know. Now see what a great guy he is!'

With a heart that had been splintered into a million pieces and only partially restored, Caryn acknowledged that Vance was a great guy.

In response to Caryn's questioning, Tami confirmed that she was involved with Mike, although they had no definite plans beyond a day-to-day relationship. Then she hurried off to call her brothers and confront her mother, leaving Caryn alone with a turmoil of thoughts and emotions and physical longings.

Caryn believed what she'd told Tami, and had no choice but to try to continue to act accordingly. It could never work between her and Vance, and attempting otherwise would only mean more torment and pain eventually for both of them.

Love is a four-letter word, Caryn rued to herself.

CHAPTER TWELVE

The turmoil within Caryn didn't adversely affect her work, although she often felt she performed her duties as mechanically as a robot. She almost wished she could become a robot, not in need of love, only a couple of drops of oil now and then.

With all the extra hours Caryn had voluntarily worked to try to divert her mind from Vance, the project was progressing very well.

Though the reception was poor and the music was obviously taped, since the same tunes repeated at approximately the same time each morning, Caryn had recently acquired the habit of switching on a transistor radio before leaving the cottage, trying to drown out her thoughts and feelings with its noise.

Today she was barely listening to the chatter of the five-minute news, perking up her ears only momentarily when the announcer mentioned a strong earthquake the previous evening in Alaska—8.2 on the Richter scale. She was interested, having lived in Alaska for a while with her father, and was glad to learn the quake had struck only an uninhabited region of the far north.

She received her personal earth-shattering news when she arrived at the field office, rushing inside to respond to the telephone's insistent jangling.

Jordan Nash announced that John Umeshi was filing a lawsuit against Resorts Inc. and Caryn, charging her with sexual harassment.

Caryn made a perfunctory, surprised reply before Jordan continued: 'I doubt that Umeshi really expects to get anywhere with his action, except to stir up trouble. I suspect he's figured out by now that Resorts Inc. has made his character known to the other contractors on the islands.'

Caryn was already constructing her case. Kano would testify on her behalf, but the other workers didn't know anything definite one way or the other. There was one unimpeachable witness as to who actually had harassed whom—if Vance would allow himself still to believe his own eyes, and if he wasn't so angry or apathetic toward her that he'd refuse to help.

The first step was a hearing before the Equal Employment Opportunity Commission, though John Umeshi already had retained an attorney to file a civil court suit also.

Caryn listened while Jordan continued to assure her of his and the company's support and trust, explaining they'd have one of the best lawyers in Honolulu represent her. 'This isn't good for the corporate image, though.

204

Not good at all, which I'm sure is what Umeshi wants, damn him. Maybe we should consider some quiet financial settlement with him.'

'No,' Caryn, roused out of her initial stupor, practically shouted into the phone. 'I'm fighting this with or without the company's support. You make any kind of private settlement with Umeshi, and you've got my resignation.'

Jordan stalled by clearing his throat before saying, 'I was afraid you'd feel like that. Okay, Caryn, we do it your way.'

They discussed generalities about the project before Jordan closed with, 'Oh, by the way, we've named the resort—getting ready to launch the preopening publicity, you know. We're calling it The Tradewinds.'

That was the first amusing thing Caryn had heard in days. She was genuinely laughing as she hung up the receiver. The Tradewinds. She'd like to trade them all right, for anything, anytime, anyplace.

With agitation and impatience, she bided time until the day's postal delivery. The offending documents arrived by certified mail.

Caryn took them with her to show to Vance. He was her best hope.

Exasperated with herself for caring, she detoured by her cottage to shower and change into a simple ivory sundress.

Clutching the manila envelope containing the legal documents, she rang the doorbell at

Vance's house. Hira answered.

'I'd like to talk to Vance.'

Hira smiled joyfully, misunderstanding Caryn's visit. 'He's having lunch in the dining room. Go right in.' She didn't bother to announce Caryn.

Caryn stepped hesitantly into the cherry-wood paneled room where she and Vance had shared a candlelight dinner and other intimacies not so long ago. Scenes from that evening replayed in her mind as she studied Vance from behind—the thick chestnut hair, the tanned neck, the broad shoulders.

Moving toward him, she had just prepared to speak when he pushed back his chair, stood, and turned. His query was one of soft surprise: 'Caryn, what are you doing here?'

She felt as if she could drown in the silver pools of his eyes. Seeing him so close, his handsome features so well defined in the sunlight flowing through the glass door, she almost couldn't talk. The words came out haltingly, 'I'm here because I need you—'

Vance enveloped her before she could finish her sentence, crushing her in a tight embrace, and Caryn knew she never wanted to leave the circle of his arms—never. Her palms rested flat against his muscular chest, and she couldn't summon the emotional strength to urge him away.

His lips hovered above hers. 'Darling, I've been waiting for you to come...'

If she kissed him, she'd be lost forever. All her reasons for avoiding Vance were still valid, she tried to convince herself.

She couldn't speak coherently if she continued to look at him. She drew away and turned her back on him.

Vance's arms enfolded her from behind, his hands melting her to liquid fire. She had to lean back against his wonderful, powerful body for a moment, just a second...

His lips toyed with the sensitive lobe of her ear before he murmured, 'Darling, what's wrong? Why did you turn away?'

Her mouth was so dry that a reply was almost impossible. Seconds seemed to stretch to infinity before she managed, 'Vance, you don't understand. I came here on business.'

He released her immediately, and she felt the rending loss of his body torn from hers. She still couldn't bring herself to look at him, feeling like an inane schoolgirl. She explained in skeletal terms as she extracted the papers, 'John Umeshi's suing me for sexual harassment leading to his termination. I hoped you'd be willing to testify about witnessing his attempted assault on me to help clear up this matter.'

The thundering silence that followed her request devastated Caryn. At last she had to swivel to search Vance's features for an answer. His knuckles showed white on tightened fists, and his face was the embodiment of raw fury, which he masked when he realized she was looking at him. His verbal response was cool and businesslike: 'Of course.'

He examined the papers. 'I know this EEO officer, and I've met Umeshi's attorney. I'll fly to Honolulu this afternoon and straighten this out.'

'I appreciate that. Thank you very much,' Caryn said formally.

'You're welcome.' Vance's voice seemed to issue from a void—detached, emotionless.

Caryn couldn't bring herself to return to the job right away. She'd earned some time off, and Kano could easily supervise the afternoon's work. She had a lot of thinking and sorting out to do without further delay.

The vibrancy, the chemistry, the passion— yes, the love—that she and Vance shared together were real. She'd just been reminded of that, not that she'd ever been able to forget.

Was she being a fool to ignore the rapturous realities that could be today because of vague apprehensions about tomorrow?

After apprising Kano of her general plans, Caryn put on a bikini and a short lacy cover-up, then loaded her recently acquired windsurfing gear onto her rented Toyota.

She had to turn the ignition key and pump the gas several times before the engine agreed to roar fully into action. She'd been having that trouble for the last few days, so she should take the car into Kaunakakai right now.

But hanging around a greasy garage wasn't what she had in mind for her afternoon off. Instead, she drove the opposite direction, toward her special beach. She wanted to be alone with her thoughts, to concentrate. So she didn't even switch on the radio during the course of her hour's drive.

Caryn noticed a Coast Guard cutter heading the other way around the curve of the island as she neared her special beach.

* * *

Vance banked the Beechcraft as he approached WindsEnd. There was no sign of people. That was good. They had followed his instructions.

The plane whirred down the airstrip. He expertly brought it to a stop just short of the hangar, and was about to taxi inside when he saw Kano running toward him, waving his arms.

Vance cut the engines and disentangled his long legs from the aircraft. He jumped down as Kano neared. 'Kano, what are you doing here? Everybody should have headed for higher ground by now.'

'I'm glad you're back,' Kano puffed, trying to muster enough breath to continue after his long run.

'My employees have standing orders to evacuate whenever there's a tsunami warning, no matter how remote the possibility. They're to take along as much livestock as they can round up within a reasonable margin of safety, then *go*! You resort people had better get your crews moving up toward the hills too.'

Kano had recovered enough breath to speak. 'Everybody's gone but me. I've been on the telephone to other parts of the island, and on the radio to some of the fishing boats that were still out.'

As Kano gulped in another dose of air, Vance asked, 'Why?'

'Caryn—we can't find her anywhere. She left late this morning with her windsurfing gear, but she didn't say exactly where she was going. She could be at any of a hundred beaches anywhere on the island.'

Icy fear clenched and compressed Vance's heart. His own voice sounded unfamiliar, as if issuing from a stranger. He tried to convince himself, to grasp hope. 'She probably heard the warning. She's probably safe.' But already he was climbing back into the plane.

'Nobody I've talked to has seen her. And the boats are all coming back in now.'

'The tsunami probably won't hit WindsEnd. Those big waves tend to gather into the low valleys and curved bays, like Halawa in '46. But you go on, get to higher ground just in case. If Caryn's still out there, I'll find her.'

I have to find her. I won't lose her now, not like this.

Kano was insisting, 'I'm staying here by the radio.' They agreed on a frequency.

'Any guess where I should start?'

Kano shook his head in quiet desperation. 'West, I suppose. The road east to Halawa is so bad. I taught her to windsurf at the beaches west of here.'

As he taxied for takeoff, Vance thought of Halawa, the place where they'd been so happy that one afternoon. No, of course not. She didn't want to relive any memories of him, didn't revel in those reminiscences the way he did. Why should she?

She'd never said she loved him, and never would say it now after the way he'd verbally assaulted her, time and again. Especially that last time—such terrible denouncement when she'd been willing to give herself to him and to absorb everything that was his to give in return.

Vance headed the plane west, maintaining a slow speed while he tried to scan for a tall, lithe figure, a silken mass of tawny hair against the golden sands. Skimming as low as possible, he followed each curve and contour of the island, as he had longed to travel and explore every contour and recess of Caryn's supple, beloved form.

How could he have hurled such horrible accusations at the woman he loved, loved so very much. *Pride goeth before a fall*—a snatch of Sunday School reprised across his mind. His pride, his damned masculine pride. He'd thought it best that it ended before she could hurt him. But no agony could be greater than the constant torture he'd endured every minute since Caryn had refused his love.

God, please... whether he could have her for a lifetime, or a year, or a month, or an hour, he'd cherish every millisecond of that period, and nourish the memory for the rest of eternity. He'd never regret spending what time he could with her, and he wouldn't try to hold her whenever she wanted to leave.

The azure sea seemed beautiful and calm as usual. Vance passed the small harbor at Kaunakakai, skimmed past the coconut grove planted by King Kamehameha, and rounded Kepuhi Beach and the temporarily abandoned Sheraton resort at the west end of Molokai, not even glancing at the vague outline of Honolulu across the channel.

He shunted past the high *pali*, over the once notorious shores of Kalaupapa. Then he was passing the area of high cliffs and lush jungle at the northeast side of the island, only accessible to the hardiest hikers or by boat during the rare periods when the winds consented. Caryn couldn't be here.

The entire outer fringe of Molokai seemed deserted. Maybe partly because the peak tourist season was past and this was a workday for most residents, and partly because the sophisticated tsunami warning system had alerted everyone in time.

Caryn was all right. He'd see her again. And the hell with his pride—he'd go down on his knees to beg her forgiveness.

Vance wanted to share his relief. He contacted Kano on the radio, 'I've covered three-quarters of the island, and there's nobody out here. Caryn must be safe.'

Why hadn't Caryn telephoned WindsEnd to let them know she was all right? Kano said he'd been by the telephone. Didn't she know people would be worried about her? Besides, she had a management responsibility to make sure her own crews were safely evacuated.

The burst of anger that followed in the wake of his anguished worry over Caryn spent itself as quickly as it had erupted.

His eyes wavered to the shimmering ribbon of Moaula Falls as he rounded the eastern curve of the island, certain the Halawa Valley would be as deserted as the rest of Molokai's coastal areas.

*   *   *

Caryn's head broke the water just as the plane passed over. The capricious winds had playfully dunked her into the sea for the third time that afternoon. She prepared to climb back onto her two-by-eleven-foot board and haul the sail back out of the ocean.

He'd been right. Halawa would have been the last place she'd go. There was no one on the beach and no sail billowing in the breeze.

Just one more stretch to check, less than 20 percent of the shoreline remaining, before he could return to WindsEnd secure in the knowledge that Caryn was safe.

But wait! Had he missed something back there. Just a snatch of color varying the blue of the sea.

Probably his eyes playing tricks. They were feeling the strain of his concentrated search.

A few more beaches between here and WindsEnd to check—no, he'd turn back and take another look at Halawa.

There it was! A wedge of yellow floating atop the deceptively placid, cerulean sea. But what was it? Vance banked to circle again, bringing the plane even lower as he grabbed the binoculars.

He saw something. Maybe a sailboard. Then a slender creamy limb extending out of the ocean.

Could it be Caryn? Whoever it was, that person was in danger and he'd try to help. But please, let it be anybody but Caryn.

Strips of turquoise divided the tall, lithe body into three sections—a turquoise bikini that blended with the ocean as if to camouflage her.

214

Vance's heart wrenched as he recognized Caryn.

How could he warn her? There was no place to land. The road was too curvy. He'd try landing on the beach, even though it was too short and soft.

With all his mental strength, Vance battled the onslaught of emotions that threatened to inundate him. His chance of landing here in one piece was very poor. He couldn't help Caryn if he crashed.

Caryn looked up, shielding her eyes with her hand, as he flew over again.

Vance tried a series of maneuvers, crisscrossing overhead as fast and as low as possible, seesawing the wings back and forth to try to convey his desperate message.

Caryn recognized the plane, smiled, and waved every time he passed.

Oh God! She thought he was just playing games or showing off.

He'd have to get to her some other way. Driving the highway, even if he absorbed every pothole, would take too long. He flicked the switch on the radio microphone again. 'Kano, please see that the powerboat is gassed up, turned on, and ready to go. I'll be landing in a few minutes.'

Vance was sprinting toward the ocean and WindsEnd's small pier before the plane's propellers had even stopped turning. Kano waited with the purring powerboat, its well-tuned motor impatient to surge into action. In tidbits of sentences, Vance related the situation to Kano, insisting that there was nothing more Kano could do and that he should now hurry to higher ground. Despite his concern and misgivings, Kano agreed.

Vance embraced the coastline as he opened the motor to full power. The bow of the boat rose almost vertical to the water, and the zephyrs of passage whipped his face.

Vance passed between the Molokai shore and tiny Mokuhooniki Island at seventy miles per hour, but it seemed a snail's pace compared to the tsunami's speed of five hundred miles per hour.

*   *   *

Caryn recognized Vance's Beechcraft immediately. How had he known she was here? She delighted in the attention he was paying her, for whatever reason.

Was all the circling and signaling his way of telling her that his mission in Honolulu had been successful? Or was he trying to convey that he wanted further communication between them as much as she did?

Caryn had decided in the tranquility of the soft afternoon to discuss their entire situation with Vance. It was time they both started behaving like mature adults instead of insolent children. If things worked out, terrific. If they didn't, at least she would have tried.

Now that Vance was returning to WindsEnd, she'd hurry back too. Then a fleeting frown creased the slightly pinkish sunburn on her forehead—maybe he was just leaving for Honolulu, and that had been his airborne message to her.

The afternoon was blissful, lulling. The atmosphere had contributed much toward pacifying her turmoil and clearing her head to merge with her heart.

Even the breezes were reasonably cooperative for a change. She was infatuated with her ability to capture a bit of the wind and tame it to her purposes. She adored riding the wind's back as she skimmed across the sapphire waves sprinkled by the sun with glistening diamonds.

Caryn wanted to prolong this lovely sojourn, just another hour or so. Who could know the results of her forthcoming discussion with Vance? She might never be able to repeat the wonderful feelings of now.

It never occurred to Caryn that today's ambient breezes might have a sinister purpose, might be lulling her to complacence in the path of terrible danger.

She pulled her yellow-and-white-striped sail out of the water as she balanced herself on the board. The sail billowed with a whoosh of breath from the spirits of Molokai.

Again and again, she traveled to the

champagne sands of the shore, borne on the wind.

* * *

Caryn's sail waltzed toward the shore, dipping in the breeze, as Vance rounded into the half-moon bay of the Halawa Valley.

The predicted time was close, very close—maybe only minutes or seconds, since even modern technology could not be unerringly precise.

Cutting back on his speed, Vance whisked past her, running the boat aground, almost to the tall grass edging the sand.

Nearing the shore, Caryn was capsized in the boat's wake, her fanny splashing undecorously into the surf.

So rude and inconsiderate! A menace to society, whoever he was! Caryn prepared to yell a few choice expletives as she sputtered out the water she'd gulped so unceremoniously.

She was amazed to see Vance's forceful form leap from the boat and dash toward her. Had he dunked her on purpose? It looked as if his boat had gone out of control.

Caryn was wading through the shallows when Vance, heedless of his fine leather shoes, splashed through the water and grabbed her hand. 'What—'

'Run, Caryn! We've got to get to higher ground! A tsunami may hit here any minute!'

For once Caryn obeyed without question, only withdrawing her hand from Vance's as they neared her car so she could unpin the car key from her bikini top. Her fingers seemed faltering and fumbling.

Despite their haste, Vance's fingers were gentle as he recovered the key, then guided Caryn to scramble to the opposite side of the seat as he assumed the driver's position, his long legs cramped beneath the steering wheel.

As Vance repeatedly turned the key and depressed the gas pedal, the motor grumbled and growled, but refused to spring into action.

Caryn's face paled beneath her sunburn. Her complacence and procrastination had brought Vance to danger too. It would be her fault if he died. 'I've been having trouble starting the car for the last few days,' she said tremulously.

The next twist of the key brought not the slightest sound from the engine.

Vance already was launching himself out of the Toyota, reaching back to extract Caryn. 'We can't wait. We've got to get out of here.'

Vance's eyes flicked over their alternatives. He hesitated only a moment, weighing their two choices. Halawa's former residents had watched the last tsunami from the hill rising in the distance at the apex of the paved highway. At that edge of the valley, the highway ascended steeply, but there was a long stretch of flat terrain to cover to that point. The trail to Moaula Falls had a gentler incline but began its slope much nearer to their current location.

'This way!' Again imprisoning her hand in his own, Vance sprinted toward the dirt trail.

They conserved their breath for running. Though Caryn was in top physical condition, she was no match for Vance's power. It almost seemed as if he were dragging her along. She knew she was holding him back. Finally, she exhaled the words, 'You can go faster alone. Go on without me.'

Without slowing, Vance turned from his half pace ahead, and despite their peril, a smile blazed across his handsome features. 'I'm never going anywhere without you, Caryn Tallis, if I have a choice.'

Her heart soared as they continued onward, Vance towing her behind him. If only her body could join her heart on Cloud Nine, they wouldn't have to keep up this killing speed.

Caryn was puffing raggedly, 'Couldn't we ... couldn't we'—she noticed a tall palm slanted nearby—'climb that palm tree.' She'd seen a man shinny up one in a tourist show in Honolulu. It had seemed simple enough for him.

Without even looking Vance quashed, 'No, the roots are too shallow. A tsunami would rip it out of the ground.' His breath was coming harder now too, but at least he had some left.

Still, he propelled them forward, gradually upward. Caryn's lungs were scorched for air, and a pain sliced through her abdomen. Her legs felt quiveringly weak. Still, she tried to proceed, tried to...

On the verge of collapse, she barely managed to gasp, 'Vance, I can't go on.'

'Yes you can, darling. You must.' Again Vance turned as he encouraged her.

She saw his gray eyes flood with terror and dismay. Already guessing what sight she would confront, Caryn pivoted slightly. A silent scream tore at her throat.

Barreling into the bay with explosive fury was a watery monster. The wave loomed from one side of the half-moon-shaped crescent to the other. At least eight stories high, Caryn's architecturally oriented brain cataloged it peripherally.

In a heartbeat Vance pulled her off the path and threw her frontally against the nearest tree, shouting, 'Hold on to that kukui for dear life! Don't let go, no matter what happens!'

Caryn wrapped her arms as far as possible around the rough trunk, practically digging her fingernails into it. Vance's muscular body impressed against her from behind as he locked both Caryn and the tree into a simultaneous embrace.

With her profile so tightly confined against the tree that she could barely move her lips, Caryn managed to say, 'I love you, Vance. I love you.'

'At least we're together' was all Vance had time to reply before the wave struck.

At first it only gurgled around their ankles. Then it boiled up violently, slapping them even harder against the tree trunk.

God, please, no ... not now ... if it has to be, just take me, not Vance. But there was little possibility that the tsunami could claim her alone, since Vance had placed himself between them. *Please, God, please ...*

The water, cold and savage, rampaged around Caryn's waist. Higher, covering her breasts. Vance's full length remained compressed against her.

For a long moment, the chill liquid stood still. Then suddenly as it had arrived, the water receded in a rush, like a locomotive charging full speed out of the station, posing still more danger.

The departing train of water was determined to acquire two passengers. Exerting incredible pull and suction, it attempted to drag Caryn and Vance off their feet and transport them out to sea, to consign them forever to the murky ocean depths.

Vance expended most of his own substantial strength in a power play with the voracious tsunami. Caryn felt his arms slipping away, felt his body slipping away as the water forced its way between them, as he wrestled against the vortex hungry to engulf them.

No, no ... Caryn couldn't know whether she cried aloud or whether her plea merely reverberated through the corridors of her own mind.

Was the nightmare ended at last? Caryn stood, heaving for breath and control, still fastened against the kukui tree. Then she felt Vance's arms slipping away again, felt his body separate from hers.

'No!' This time it was a shouted command, to whom it may concern. Caryn released her own hold on safety to try to grasp Vance's wrists, to try to pull him back.

'It's okay, darling, it's all right,' Vance's deep voice assured, 'it's over.'

As she turned, he gathered her into his arms, murmuring, 'Oh, if I'd lost you, Caryn, if I'd lost you!'

They locked their arms about each other, clinging together for support, for life, as intensely as they had clung to the kukui tree. Vance's chin nestled against her forehead as she pressed her cheek into his shoulder, her lips almost vibrating with the pulsating of his warm throat.

For many minutes, they remained in that desperate, yet quiet and secure, embrace—not moving, not speaking, dissolving together as each revered the other, as they indulged in the wonderful feeling of each other, as they silently thanked God and celebrated the miracles of life and love.

Vance spoke first, softly, 'That statement you made—were those just "last words," or did you mean them?'

'I meant them, Vance, with all my being. I love you.' She tried to squeeze him even harder. 'I love you so much.'

'And I love you.' His arms, weary from the struggle against the tsunami, found the strength to press her even closer, fusing them together. 'Can you forgive me for being an overbearing idiot?'

'If you can forgive me for being so stubborn, for not accepting your apology and your love sooner.' Blue eyes luminous with unshed tears of happiness were raised to his. 'I'm sorry I kept us apart.'

They kissed then, gently, tenderly, deeply. A kiss that engulfed their hearts and their souls as well as their bodies.

Then Vance said, 'We'd better move still higher. Sometimes a series of tsunami hit, hours apart.'

As they partially separated, reluctantly, Caryn saw with a gasp the havoc that remained in the wake of the tsunami.

Vance gently spiraled her, placing his arm around her shoulders. 'Don't look back, darling. Never look back. Not at the physical damage caused by the tsunami, not at the emotional destruction we tried to wreak on each other.'

Then he noticed the state of her normally smooth skin, most of which had been exposed due to the brevity of her bikini. Every crevice and wrinkle and ridge of the kukui bark was etched and embossed on the once satiny canvas of her body. There were scratchy abrasions and shadows of beginning bruises. Vance touched her tenderly as a butterfly's wings as his eyes paid no less homage to her temporarily defaced form. 'Sweetheart, what have I done? I've hurt you.'

Caryn smiled comfortingly. 'You saved my life, you silly man. And at considerable risk to your own.' She caressed his beloved cheek with her hand, but he swiveled his head and pressed his lips against her palm, saying, 'Living wouldn't have meant much without you.'

Arms about each other, they started up the trail, maintaining a fairly brisk pace.

'What about Kano, Hira, the other workers and people at WindsEnd?' Caryn worried aloud.

'The people were all safe. I doubt that the resort or WindsEnd was struck anyway.' His hand tightened against her skin as he continued, 'About WindsEnd, I've been thinking about ways to make it more livable.'

Caryn chuckled, 'More livable? It's practically a mansion now.'

'But an isolated one. If we put a dish antenna on top of the hill, we could probably pick up all the Honolulu television channels. And we could buy videotapes of all the latest movies as soon as they're available. The library's already quite extensive, but you can order every book ever published if you want to. And subscribe to every magazine. We can fly to Honolulu at least once a week—'

Caryn interrupted softly, 'I don't need all that, Vance. I only need you.'

He paused and studied the ground before them. A frown furrowed his brow, and she reached up to stroke it away with a delicate touch before he said, 'I wish that were true. I know you mean it now, but in the long run, you'll need more. You'll want a career too.'

Caryn rotated her head back, her tawny hair brushing his arm. She tried to force herself to think clearly, logically. It was impossible with Vance so near. Eventually, she acknowledged the possibility of other needs with a mere wisp of a whisper: 'Maybe.'

'The tsunami didn't wipe out all the potential problems,' Vance pointed out softly.

'But now we know for sure that we love each other.'

'Was there ever really any doubt of that?'

A long moment drifted after Vance's question before it was answered in unison by both: 'Yes, I wasn't sure you loved me.' Then together they uttered a soft, astonished 'Oh' before smiling and indulging in a lingering embrace and kiss.

Caryn's lips murmured against Vance's, 'To think that we hurt and withdrew from each other so much, so unnecessarily.'

'Together we managed to make us both miserable.'

'One night I figured out that love is a four-letter word,' Caryn admitted.

'We can fix that by hyphenating s-e-x onto the end.'

Caryn laughed merrily. Then she asked demurely, 'Will we get to high enough ground to start hyphenating soon?'

'Want to run again?'

'Oh no. After all, we have a lifetime.'

'Do we? We still have some things to discuss.'

'I suppose so,' she sighed. But she didn't want to confront phantoms of possible future difficulties now. Now she only wanted Vance. Like Scarlett O'Hara, tomorrow she'd think about 'that,' whatever 'that' was.

'First, I want you to know that I won't try to hold you if ever you decide to leave.'

'I want you to plan on holding me always, forever.' Her sapphire eyes sparkled with love.

A five-hundred-watt smile blazed across his features. 'I'll be glad to oblige.' He emphasized the words by tightening his arm around her waist. 'But there's more.'

Aware only of Vance's powerful closeness, of her desperate need for him, Caryn couldn't respond in the next moment.

Vance persisted. 'I've watched you, more than you know. You're good at your job and, most importantly, you enjoy it. I can't ask you to give that up entirely and stay at WindsEnd twenty-four hours a day.'

Caryn's total being shattered into billions of infinitesimal pieces. He said he loved her, but he still didn't want her to share his life, even though she'd be the one who'd have to make most of the adjustments.

Unaware that she felt annihilated, Vance was saying, 'I thought of involving you in the management of WindsEnd, along with me, but I'm sure you don't want to go through life as second-in-command of everything. Besides, that's not your chosen field. So I've come up with an alternate solution, even though the major compromise will still be yours.'

Caryn resurrected a little.

Vance's eyes searched hers, eager for an honest reaction. 'I know it can't compare to working all over the entire world, but there's a lot of construction on the other Hawaiian islands, not so much as a few years ago, but enough to keep a top-notch construction superintendent busy.'

Caryn felt uplifted, rapturous already, as Vance continued: 'I figured we could buy another plane—I know most families just have two cars—but I could teach you to fly, and you could commute to projects on Oahu and Maui. Even Kauai or the Big Island wouldn't take any longer than a normal urban commute in rush-hour traffic.'

Caryn clasped her hands around his neck, laughing in delight, not only with her lips but with every cell of her body and her mind.

'Darling, I won't even need a plane to fly, if I'm coming home to you.'

They kissed again, exploring and probing with a promise of the deeper merging to come, mutually molding to each other. 'When we get to higher ground,' he murmured huskily, his breath feathery in her ear, 'I may keep you up there for days.'

'I don't want to ever come back down to earth anyway,' was her teasing reply.

'Soon we'll be joined into one, for now, for always. You'll be the other half of me, and I the other half of you, for all time.'

Belonging with Vance. Half of one with Vance. Therefore belonging to Molokai, the winds seemed to realize, to understand, to accept.

Caryn could sense a change as the breezes caressed her, tender, welcoming.

We hope you have enjoyed this Large Print book. Other Chivers Press or G. K. Hall Large Print books are available at your library or directly from the publishers. For more information about current and forthcoming titles, please call or write, without obligation, to:

Chivers Press Limited
Windsor Bridge Road
Bath BA2 3AX
England
Tel. (01225) 335336

OR

G. K. Hall
P.O. Box 159
Thorndike, Maine 04986
USA
Tel. (800) 223–6121 (U.S. & Canada)
In Maine call collect: (207) 948–2962

All our Large Print titles are designed for easy reading, and all our books are made to last.